HEALER GANG

E.D.G. SMITH

A NOTE ABOUT AMERICAN INDIANS

The word *Injun* has been used as a derogatory term for American Indians since the early 1800s. While the word *Injun* is no longer acceptable, the term would have been used on the Colorado frontier of the 1880s. This is the period of the Benton Series.

I have restricted the use of the word *Injun* in the Benton Series to the speech of the villains and uneducated characters. Conversely, I have reserved use of the word *Indian* to the Bentons and other respectable characters. To have Brad or Audrey talk about *Native Americans* would be as absurd as to have them talk about snail mail.

CHAPTER 1

Sunday 28 March, 1881: "The first one to the corral gets the biggest piece of pie," challenged Audrey, reining Blaze to a halt.

"On the count of three," replied her brother, stopping his horse, Ebony, beside her.

The horses sensed the excitement of another race. Ebony bobbed her head, and Blaze gave a quick snort. The quarter-mile lane to the corral would go quickly. The spring sun invigorated the horses and their riders.

"One, two, three," counted Audrey loudly, leaning forward in her saddle. The horses bolted forward and galloped toward the corral gate.

"A tie," declared Brad, as Ebony stopped inside the corral. Instead of dismounting, he sat silently in the saddle, looking over at the house.

Looking over her saddle, Audrey teased, "If you stay on your horse, I'll eat both pieces of pie."

"The back door is open!" exclaimed Brad, dismounting slowly. "I know I closed it before we went to church."

"I know you did," confirmed Audrey, suddenly attentive to her brother's words, "because I checked it, too."

Leaving their horses in the corral, they went to the

back door. As they reached the open door, they heard their parents' buggy approach.

"We'd better wait for Pa," cautioned Brad.

"I'll get him," said Audrey, running to the buggy.

Audrey quickly explained what they had seen. Harold Benton jumped down, looped the reins over the corral rail, and ran to the back door with his daughter. They slowly entered the house; their father stopped, listened, and looked around the kitchen.

"The pie is missing," said Brad in a whisper.

"Nana's skillet and stew pot are missing, too," said Audrey.

Their father reached under his winter coat on the coat hook, removed his gun belt, and strapped it on. Drawing his pistol, he slowly walked into the parlor.

"No one is here," said Brad. "They probably robbed us while we were at church."

"I believe you're right, but I'll check upstairs anyway," replied his father.

A few minutes later, all five Bentons were in the kitchen talking about the robbery.

"The apple-blackberry pie, my best skillet, and the stew pot are gone," said Victoria, Brad and Audrey's grandmother. Nana, as they called her, had come to Riverton to help their mother just before Audrey's birth and had remained. Her husband had been killed in the Civil War.

"Check your rooms," ordered their mother. "If he, or they, took the pie and stew pot, they probably searched every room for valuables. After you've checked your rooms, we'll all meet here and talk about Sunday dinner."

Brad opened his chest of drawers, found everything

there, and then checked his closet, only to find that his new rifle was missing. "Pa, my rifle is gone."

"Harold," said his wife, "the gold locket you gave me at our wedding is missing."

"I don't think I'm missing anything," said Audrey.

"I'm not missing anything, either," said Nana. "The Bible my father gave me as a wedding present is the only thing of value that I have, and that is sentimental value. The thief, or thieves, certainly weren't looking for the word of the Lord."

"Let's discuss this at Sunday dinner, without the pie," said their father grimly.

Nana nodded at Brad, "bring up some vegetables. I'll make biscuits, since they also took the bread I'd baked. The roast is still in the oven. They smelled the pie and bread and ignored the roast."

"Amen," said their father, concluding the blessing.

"Don't let the burglary ruin our Sunday dinner," commanded Nana.

"I won't," said Brad.

Harold Benton cut slices of roast beef and placed a slice on the plate his wife, Abby, held. She passed the plate to Audrey, who passed it to Brad, who passed it to Nana. By the time he placed a slice on his own plate, the rest of the family had already helped themselves to the biscuits and vegetables.

"Nana," said Brad, "You were right when you said the thieves weren't looking for the word of the Lord, because they took a real mix of things: they took my rifle, a pie, Ma's locket, the new skillet, the stewpot, and the bread."

"It is an odd assortment, but logical," she observed. "The rifle and gold locket can be sold. They took the food because they were hungry, and the skillet and pot either because they needed them or because they can also be easily sold."

"Then they're probably new to the area," concluded Audrey.

"Or passing through," added their mother. "I hope they're passing through, I wouldn't want to have more things stolen."

"I'll talk to Sheriff Tate first thing Monday morning," said their father. "There is nothing he can do about the theft today. Brad and I looked but didn't find any unique horse or wagon tracks."

"A few weeks without rain make it hard to see any horse or wagon tracks, even unique tracks," added Brad. "I don't think even Running Bear could find the thief's tracks."

"Is the ground really that hard?" asked Audrey.

"It is on the road," confirmed Nana, as she saw Brad eat the last bite of roast from his plate. "The thief would have come down the lane to the house, not through the pasture. We destroyed his tracks when we came home."

"Pa, may I have another slice of roast?" Brad interrupted, passing his plate to his grandmother's waiting hand.

Nana added two biscuits to Brad's plate while Harold cut a thick slice of roast beef for his son.

"Thank you," said Brad, taking the plate.

She continued, "Everything that was taken is

replaceable. The skillet, pot, and rifle are easy to replace. The locket will be more difficult, but I'll ask Sheriff Tate to wire a description of it and its engraving to Denver. Denver is the closest place where they could sell jewelry."

"Harold," said Abby, her eyes moist, but with a strong voice. "I have you, despite Duke Badger's attempt on your life. The locket reminds me of our courtship and marriage, beautiful memories. But," her voice briefly quavered, then she continued firmly, "the memories are there forever, even without the locket."

Brad and Audrey said nothing as they studied their parents. Their memories of searching for their father last October, after the sheriff's posse had failed to find him, were indelibly imprinted in their minds.

"Henry took care of that, that beast!" spat Nana. "That despicable monster, Duke Badger, got just what he deserved."

Duke Badger had held up the stagecoach that Brad, Audrey, and their father were taking to Denver. When Duke discovered that the stage had no gold, he took their father with him. The next day Sheriff Tate and his posse began an unsuccessful three-day search. Brad and Audrey left the next day searching for their father on their own.

"I remember seeing two wolves drop dead in front of me," recalled their father. "I kept my eyes on the other wolves. When I saw two more wolves drop, I knew the help I had prayed for had arrived."

Duke Badger had taken their father's hat, coat, and boots before wounding him. Then, laughing, he had ridden off, leaving their father to the wolves.

"You taught us how to shoot, Pa," comforted Audrey, gripping her father's hand. "We aimed and gently squeezed the trigger, just like you told us."

"That was excellent marksmanship," confirmed Nana. "I believe it was half a mile."

"It wasn't that far," commented Brad, "It was only about 200 yards."

"It was over a quarter of a mile," corrected their father. "And," he paused, "it was starting to snow and the wind was blowing."

"We found you in time, Pa," said Audrey. "That is what really counts. We found you before the blizzard or the wolves got you."

"And we just missed tangling with Duke Badger," added Brad.

Brad and Audrey bandaged their father's wound and built a shelter as the blizzard was starting. Three days later, they rode into Riverton with their father and a member of Duke Badger's gang that they had captured.

"I'll talk to Buckley Hodges Monday about your rifle," said his father. "The thieves may try to sell it locally, and he has the serial number, since he sold it to me."

"Buckley?" asked Audrey.

"Yes," replied their father, "Buckley. Buck Jr. is getting to be a young man, and folks are confusing their names, so Mr. Hodges is asking everyone to call him Buckley, and his son, Buck."

"That will help," agreed Brad. "New people won't have to ask, 'Jr. or Sr.' It will eliminate the junior or senior question."

"If your rifle doesn't show up in a few weeks, we can

order another one," encouraged Audrey. "We have more than enough reward money in the bank."

"Yes, we can order another one," agreed their father.

"Enough of this talk about outlaws and thieves," announced Nana. "We need to clean the table, do the chores and you two need to do your homework. I think I'll bake another pie, too. I'd like a piece before I go to bed tonight, how about you, Brad?"

"I'll get the apples and blackberries from the cellar," said Brad, rapidly pushing his chair back from the table.

"I think that means he'd like some pie," laughed his mother, gently patting her son on the back as he left the table.

"Supper is ready," announced their mother. "Hot tea, coffee, milk, roast beef sandwiches, and two apple-blackberry pies."

After a brief grace, Audrey poured coffee for her father while Nana poured tea for everyone else. Brad wasted no time and immediately began devouring his sandwich.

"I made a second sandwich for you, Brad," said Nana. "I thought you might have an appetite after chopping all that wood and kindling."

"Thank you," replied Brad.

"Pa, do you think the thief, or thieves, will return?" asked Audrey.

"No, I don't think they'll come back. But we should start locking our doors. Riverton is growing, new people are moving into town, and more people are passing through."

"Everyone leaves their doors unlocked," said their mother. "You never know when someone might need shelter or food."

"I found a note from Len Reno last month," confirmed their grandmother. "His horse had gone lame while he was hunting. He hadn't eaten for about a day and walked miles to reach our place. Our house was unlocked, as usual, so he made himself a big breakfast of eggs, bacon, coffee, and some bread. To get home, he borrowed Ebony. That afternoon he rode back on his other horse, returned Ebony, and gave us a large venison roast as a thank-you present."

"You let him give you a roast for the use of Ebony?" questioned Brad.

"I couldn't very well refuse, but in return, I did give him a pie to take home," Nana replied.

"Starting tonight, we'll start locking the doors when we leave," said their father. "I have no concern about Len Reno, or most other folks. I do have a concern about the unsavory element that can come when a town grows, and Riverton is growing."

"A growing town often attracts criminal behavior," nodded Nana.

"Can't the thief just kick in the door?" asked Audrey.

"Yes, but many thieves will stop when they find the door is locked. Rather than break a window or kick in a door, they'll just go to the next house."

"Brad, will you please bring in the pie?" asked Nana.

"Right away," He pushed his chair back and hurried to the kitchen.

"We'll use our sandwich plates," said their mother. "No need to use more dishes."

Brad placed the pie in front of his grandmother with a large knife.

"A very small slice for me, please," requested their mother. Give my young man the rest of my piece."

"Thank you, Ma."

Victoria cut the pie; she put a small slice on Abby's plate, and a large one on Brad's. "Thanks, Nana," said Brad as he took the plate.

"You're starting to get some meat on your bones," observed his grandmother. "I don't want the ladies at church to start wagging their tongues about how I'm starving my grandson."

"They won't say that," laughed Harold Benton.

"Not if you keep feeding him, he is a growing boy," said Mrs. Benton. "Tomorrow will be a busy day. The principal doesn't want us to expect less from the students just because Easter Vacation is coming. Miss Jones will ask for your homework first thing in the morning."

Brad and Audrey washed the dishes, and then did their homework. As darkness fell, they said good night to their parents and Nana, then climbed the stairs to their bedrooms.

"Let's talk," whispered Brad as they reached the door to his room.

Audrey followed him in and sat on the floor beside her brother's chest of drawers, her back against the wall. Brad sat on the floor, leaned against his bed, and put his hands behind his head looking thoughtful.

"You've got a plan brewing under that black hair of yours," she said. "What is it?"

"I thought we should talk to Buck, Harry, and Wilma

Sue before school tomorrow. Harry always comes up with something when we present him with a problem. Maybe we'll be able to get an idea about who the thief might be."

"Yes," said Audrey. "But I don't want to get involved in another expedition to catch a thief."

"Why not?"

"I'd like to spend this vacation, well, vacationing. Our last three vacations have been spent chasing outlaws."

"We caught them, didn't we?" exclaimed her brother.

"Well, yes."

"That's good, isn't it?"

"Yes, but I want to make a dress and read a book during Easter Vacation. I don't have time to do it while we're going to school."

"I won't ask for your help in catching the thief," said Brad, a twinkle in his eye, "unless I really need you. I promise."

"Brad," her blue eyes flashing angrily, "You . . . you . . . exasperate me sometimes. And this is one of those times."

"Then you'll help me ask the questions," confirmed Brad, his face breaking into a smile.

"Yes, and I'll even help you capture the thief, or thieves. I'll sew a new dress on weekends, or during the summer."

"Thank you! I knew I could count on you," he said, getting up and opening the door for his sister.

"I'll see you in the morning," she said, her anger gone.

"In the morning," he replied.

CHAPTER 2

Monday 29 March 1881: Brad and Audrey left school and headed for the stage office to visit their father. Audrey spoke first, "Wilma Sue and I talked at lunch about folks new to Riverton."

"Anything unusual?" asked Brad.

"No, just that there are some new folks."

"Harry Acker said the same thing," replied Brad. "Maybe Pa will have heard something."

As they turned onto Riverton's Main Street, two seedy-looking men came riding into town. The men studied the shops intently as their horses slowly plodded down the dusty street. Brad and Audrey watched as the men came to the hitching rail in front of the Silver Dollar Saloon. They slowly dismounted, studied Bevins's General Store, and then went into the saloon.

"I don't like the looks of those men," said Audrey.

"I don't either," said Brad. "Let's stop and talk with Sheriff Tate before we see Pa."

"He's probably going to say that it's not against the law for two men to ride down the street looking at the stores," said Audrey. "But, let's stop and tell him anyways."

Brad opened the door to the sheriff's office, and,

holding it open for his sister, eloquently said, "After you, m'lady."

"Miss Jones must be teaching you young'uns Shakespeare," said the sheriff, looking over the top of the newspaper.

"Well, as a matter of fact, she is," admitted Audrey.

"And before you ask me, yes, your Pa talked to me about the theft at your house yesterday," said the sheriff. "Is there something else I can do for you?"

"There might be something we can do for you," replied Brad. "We were going to see Pa when we saw two men riding slowly down the street."

"We know they weren't doing anything wrong," added Audrey. "But they looked real suspicious, and they were studying the shops, especially the general store."

"They stopped at the Silver Dollar," added Brad.

"There was just something about them. And, no, I can't explain it." Then Audrey folded her arms and looked at the sheriff.

"Now I'm not saying you're right," said Sheriff Tate, leaning forward in his chair. "And I'm not saying you're wrong. There's something to be said about a person's intuition, especially a woman's."

"Thank you," replied Audrey, her face brightening.

"I stop in the Silver Dollar every night," said the sheriff. "The bartender tells me about new folks, especially men that are passing through."

"Have any new folks come to town in the past week?" asked Brad.

"There is a new couple in town," said the sheriff. "Franz and Gerda Hall. Franz is working at the livery.

His wife, Gerda, is working at the laundry. They're just a normal couple, nothing unusual."

"I'm sure you're right," said Audrey.

"We'd best be going," said Brad. "We want to see Pa and get our chores done before supper."

"Before you go, I want you to know that I do appreciate you Pinkertons telling me about those men. Your instincts and recommendations have helped in the past. Now hurry on and say hello to your Pa for me."

Brad held the door open for his sister as they left the sheriff's office. They quickened their pace and crossed the street to the stage depot.

"Is school is over already?" questioned their father, looking at the large mahogany Regulator clock on the wall.

"Pa, we saw some seedy-looking men riding down the street," said Audrey. "I think they're going to cause trouble."

"I agree," said Brad. "There was something about the way they looked at the general store, the way they acted, the way they dressed, and their six-shooters were slung low."

"You're describing drifters, saddle tramps," said their father. "But that doesn't mean that they're bad men. They could simply be men that have been on the road for a long time."

"We know," said Audrey. "They're innocent until proven guilty."

"I'll ask my men about your seedy characters, and we can discuss it at dinner tonight," said their father. "But it's getting close to supper time, so you two had best be heading home."

"Yes, Pa," said Brad, opening the door.

"We'll have to hurry," remarked his sister, starting down the boardwalk at a fast pace. Brad lengthened his stride and quickly fell in beside her.

"That cornbread was superb," declared Brad as he finished his third piece.

"Wait until I bring out the dessert," warned his grandmother.

"Dessert, too!" lamented Audrey. "I don't think I have room for any pie."

"It's not pie tonight," said their mother. "It's oatmeal cookies."

"While Victoria is serving the cookies, I'll tell you what I learned about your two seedy men," said their father. "Jim Bates heard that the men were going to be staying in town for a while. They're looking for work to earn some money before they move on."

"You don't sound like you believe that explanation," observed Abby.

"Jim said the men didn't sound truthful, but one of the men, Willy Brown, did accept his suggestion to check at the livery."

The family fell into a deep discussion before their mother interrupted, "It's time to do the dishes and homework. I don't want any slacking off just because Easter Vacation is next week. And I have some papers to grade."

Brad and Audrey collected the dishes, and Nana began wrapping the cornbread for tomorrow's lunches. Once the table was cleared, Harold sat down again.

He carefully emptied his pistol, and began cleaning it. Abby sat down at the other end of the oak table and began grading her students' papers.

Brad looked at his sister as he dried a plate. "Audrey, do you still think those two men are up to no good?"

"Yes, but I hope I'm wrong."

"We can ask Harry, Buck, and Wilma Sue tomorrow," said Brad. "Maybe their parents talked about the men tonight, too."

By the time they had finished the dishes, their father had finished cleaning his pistol and was in his chair reading. Audrey and Brad sat down at the table and started to study.

Sometime later, Audrey closed her book, looking bored and a little sleepy. "Pa, what time is it?"

He pulled out his pocket watch, angled it toward the kerosene lamp, and said, "A little after eight."

"Bedtime," announced Brad, closing his book, and then paused. "Pa, did Hank Lacy come into town today?"

"No, but he should be at church Sunday. He rarely misses two Sundays in a row. And, I'm sure he can use you and Audrey for a day or two during Easter Vacation."

"Just checking," said Brad, starting up the stairs. "Good night, Pa, Ma, Nana."

"Same for me," said Audrey. "I'll see you in the morning."

CHAPTER 3

Sunday Morning: Wilma Sue Bevins and Buck Hodges stood in front of the church and waved at Brad and Audrey. Brad and his sister stopped, dismounted, and looped their reins over the hitching rail.

"Good morning," greeted Audrey as she and Brad reached the front steps. "The two of you are here early."

"One more week of school, and then we have a week off," said Buck. "What are the Bentons going to do?"

"We might find out today," replied Brad. "Mr. Lacy said he might be able to use us for a few days at the Bar-X Ranch."

"Oh, and there's another new couple in town," said Wilma Sue. "I don't know their name, but Pa said they're not in good health."

They talked a few more minutes, watching their friends and neighbors stop and chat on the church steps. When the piano music started, however, folks quickly stopped talking and went inside.

"Ma's playing the prelude," said Audrey. "We'd better go in."

Brad and Audrey joined Nana and their father in their pew just before their mother started the opening hymn. As usual, Reverend Wesley sang the hymn forcefully as he strode down the aisle, which encouraged

20

the congregation to raise their voices along with him. Buckley Hodges read the lesson for the day, and then returned to join his wife and son in the congregation for the sermon.

After the sermon, Reverend Wesley left the pulpit and came down and stood in front of the first row of pews. "And now for some announcements," he said. "Two couples new to Riverton have joined the church. Franz and Gerda Hall," motioning to them with his right hand. Franz and Gerda stood up so the congregation could see them.

"And," continued the reverend, "Earl and Wenda Walker," he said, motioning to them with his left hand. "Please welcome them to Riverton and to our church family."

Earl and Wenda Walker stood up, and, like the Halls, turned around so the congregation could see them. The reverend finished his announcements and nodded to Abby. Abby played a hymn for the offertory as Jake Jackson passed the collection plate.

"Brad," whispered Audrey.

"Yes," answered Brad softly into his sister's ear.

"Two new couples, and no children."

"So?"

"Don't you think that is unusual?"

"Well, maybe they can't have children, or their children died from whooping cough, La Grippe, or something else."

"Let's talk some more after the service," whispered Audrey.

Abby played the closing hymn and Reverend Wesley proclaimed, "Let us go forth in the name of Christ."

Abby started playing the postlude, and folks greeted each other as they lined up to say hello to the reverend. Audrey pulled Brad away from the aisle so they could be alone.

"You've sure got a burr under your saddle blanket this morning," said Brad. "I take it you don't trust the two new couples, am I correct?"

"Yes, let's go talk to Wilma Sue before she leaves."

Brad followed his sister out the side door of the church and around to the front.

"Wilma Sue," said Audrey, as she saw her friend coming down the steps of the church.

"Audrey! You were behind me. How did you get out ahead of me?"

"We took the side door," said Brad. "We wanted to be sure we caught you before you left."

"You've caught me, now what can I do for you?" said Wilma Sue, putting her arm around Audrey.

"Have you heard anything more about the new people in town?"

"Wenda Walker has poor eyesight, and her husband, Earl, coughs, like he has the consumption. Wenda is working at the hotel as a maid. Earl is working at the Silver Dollar, washing dishes and scrubbing up."

"He coughs and washes dishes," said Audrey. "That's a good reason to never eat at the Silver Dollar."

"The seedy characters that have been going there recently is another good reason," added Brad.

"I know," said Wilma Sue. "One of them came into the store yesterday. He was polite, but I felt a lot better after he left. I didn't trust him."

"Wilma Sue," called Mrs. Bevins, "we have to go now."

"I'll see you at school tomorrow," she said, joining her mother. "Bye."

After Wilma Sue had walked away, Brad turned to his sister and said, "Audrey, I really believe you are overly suspicious of newcomers since we were robbed."

"Maybe I am, but I don't think all of the newcomers are genuine. Take the two drifters, and now two new couples. It doesn't look like they are going to become permanent residents of Riverton."

"You may be right," agreed Brad, looking at the buggies and buckboards in back of the church. "Pa is helping Ma and Nana into the buggy. Let's mount up and head home. Maybe they heard something."

Brad and Audrey went to the hitching rail, unlooped their reins, and mounted their horses. Brad softly clucked, and Ebony fell in behind their parents' buggy.

"Brad," asked Audrey, "do you think I'm wrong?"

"About the drifters, no; about the Halls and Walkers, I don't know. Maybe I'll be able to give you a yes or no answer in a few weeks."

"Beans and biscuits," said Harold Benton. "That was a superb meal."

Abby looked at him with a twinkle in her eye and said, "Harold, every meal that I've ever made has been superb."

"And it will always be that way," he said, giving his wife's hand a gentle squeeze.

"Pa," said Audrey, in mock seriousness. "You told me that the Army pancakes I made after we rescued you from Duke Badger were superb."

"They were," he said. "I just like beans and biscuits, too."

"Beans and biscuits is my favorite, too," said Brad, pushing his chair back from the table, "especially when there's lots of ham."

"Dish-washing time," said Audrey as she began collecting the dishes.

"I've got a few papers to grade," said their mother, passing dishes to her daughter.

Brad scraped some flakes from a bar of soap into the dishpan and then added hot water from the stove. A few pumps of cold water from the kitchen pump cooled the water enough for his hands. Audrey put the dishes in the pan and dropped the dishrag on top of them.

"I've been thinking about what Pa, Buck, and Wilma Sue said. Let's talk in your room before we go to bed," said Audrey softly, placing a plate on the counter for Brad to dry.

"I've been thinking, too," said Brad, putting a cup in the cabinet. "I've got some ideas. We can talk about it right after we finish our homework.

"I don't have that much homework," said Audrey. "I'm pretty well caught up, how about you?"

"I've got the history chapter to review again. Maybe we can head upstairs a little earlier than usual."

Later that evening, Audrey said, "I've finished my studies. Good night, everyone. See you for breakfast."

"I'm packing it in for the night, too," added Brad, closing his history book.

When they reached the top of the stairs, Audrey entered Brad's room and sat on the floor beside her brother's chest of drawers. Brad followed his sister in the room, closed the door, and sat on the floor, his back against his bed.

"What have you come up with?" he asked.

"I don't know, yet. But what we have so far are two drifters and the two couples. That's six people with no logical reason to select Riverton as their home."

"I think I see your point," said Brad. "But why shouldn't they select Riverton as a place to live?"

"They came here without a job, or the prospect of a job," said Audrey. "It doesn't make sense to go to a small town and expect to find work, especially since they came from up north. Their opportunity for employment would be much better in Denver. Denver is a rapidly growing city."

"Now I see your point," said Brad. "The Halls arrived in a covered wagon, and they rented that old house by the livery. Franz is working part-time at the livery, and Gerda is working at the laundry. Pa said that Alex asked to buy their wagon, but they said they didn't want to sell it."

"Why would they want to keep an old covered wagon if they're going to stay in Riverton?" asked Audrey.

"Meanwhile, Wenda Walker is working as a maid at the hotel. Her husband, Earl, is washing dishes and sweeping floors at the Silver Dollar."

"They're renting a small room in the attic of the saloon," said Audrey.

"And no one knows how they arrived in town. They didn't come by stage, and they have no horses," said Brad, thoughtfully stroking his chin. "I guess it is possible that they walked into town with just the clothes on their backs."

"Sure," scoffed Audrey, "and Earl Walker can walk all the way to Riverton from another town, despite his cough." She rolled her eyes.

"Audrey," said Brad.

"Yes?"

"We're becoming Pinkertons again."

"I think you're right," she replied. "Something is going on, we just don't know what it is."

"We'll just keep listening and looking for clues," said Brad. "When we get enough clues, we'll be able to figure out what it is."

"Good night, Mr. Pinkerton," giggled Audrey, opening the door.

"Good night, Miss Pinkerton, I'll see you in the morning."

CHAPTER 4

Friday, 9 April 1881: "Easter Vacation, at last," cheered Brad, as they reached the bottom of the school steps. "Let's go see Pa on the way home."

The bright afternoon sun and absence of wind prompted Brad to unbutton his coat. By the time they reached Main Street, Audrey was unbuttoning her coat as she climbed onto the boardwalk.

"A poster," remarked Audrey, stopping in front of the general store.

Dr. Jeremiah Chetham, *Healer*, will conduct a spiritual revival and healing session for the citizens of Riverton on the Saturday before Easter, seven o'clock in the evening at the school meeting room.

"I wonder what that is?" puzzled Brad.

"We can ask Pa," replied Audrey. "There's another poster."

"Miracles, afflictions removed, lameness cured," read Brad. **"Jesus needs you. Rediscover your faith the Saturday before Easter. Come to the school meeting room, seven o'clock in the evening. All invited."**

They passed several more posters on their way to the stage office. Brad opened the door, and they stepped inside. Their father was standing by the stove, drinking coffee and talking with Jim Bates, one of the stage drivers.

Jim looked up at Brad and said, "There's a good driver, Harold, and he's experienced!"

"Ready for Easter Vacation?" asked their father with a wink.

"We start by going to the Bar-X Ranch tomorrow and helping Hank Lacy," answered Audrey. "But for now, what do you know about Dr. Jeremiah Chetham, Healer?"

"Not too much. One of his advance men rented the school meeting room for next Saturday night and had the posters printed this morning. He was tacking them up all over town early this afternoon."

"Reverend Wesley has a pretty good handle on evangelists and revivalists," said Jim Bates. "You might ask him on the way home."

"We will," said Brad. "And we'll come wash the windows and clean the office early next week."

"Old Man Sun has been working a mite harder getting his light through the glass lately," observed the stage driver squinting closely at a pane of glass. "Why, the flies hardly know where the windows are anymore."

"They're not that bad," giggled Audrey. "Are they?"

"Not quite," said Brad, watching his sister make a streak on the window with her finger.

"But they are in need of a good cleaning," agreed Audrey, looking at the grime on her fingertip.

"Let's go see if Reverend Wesley is in and ask him about Dr. Chetham," said Brad, gently pulling his sister toward the door.

"We'll see you at dinner, Pa," said Audrey, as they left the stage office.

Brad closed the door and surmised, "Almost everyone has some affliction that needs curing. The meeting room will probably be packed."

"But a 'Spiritual Revival'?" wondered Audrey. "That's what Reverend Wesley and Father O'Brien do every Sunday. What can he do that they can't do?"

As they turned onto the reverend's street, they saw the posters tacked to trees. "At least they don't have posters in his front yard," muttered Brad, opening the gate.

"Or on his front porch," added Audrey.

Brad gently knocked on the door and stepped back. He heard Mrs. Wesley humming as she came to the door.

"Welcome, come in. Bob is in his office working on Sunday's sermon. He gets so engrossed in his work that he doesn't hear when someone knocks. I'll tell him you're here."

Reverend Wesley came to greet them just as soon as his wife retrieved him. "Brad, Audrey, what can I do for you?"

"We thought you might be able to tell us about Dr. Jeremiah Chetham," said Brad. "His posters are up all over town."

"I don't think I can," replied the reverend. "I haven't left the house all day. What do the posters say?"

"They say that he is a healer, performs miracles, cures lameness, and helps people rediscover their faith," said Audrey.

"Next Saturday evening in the school meeting room," added Brad.

"Sounds like an evangelist," concluded the reverend. "Some are good and some are bad."

"How can you tell if he's going to be a good one?" asked Audrey.

"You can't," laughed the reverend. "But I can wire a friend in Denver and ask if he's heard of Dr. Jeremiah Chetham."

"Who is a good evangelist?" asked Audrey.

"Dwight Moody, he's a master evangelist. He's brought many people to the Lord. His men meet with the religious leaders of a town before the meeting. When people come to him, he helps them find the Lord. Then, he sends them to the town's churches."

"How, or why, does he do that?" asked Brad.

"Let's say Mr. Moody was coming to Riverton. His advance men would meet with us ahead of time. At the meeting, he'd have men help him send folks to the right church. If a man's background was Catholic, he'd send them to Father O'Brien. If the man's background was Protestant, he'd send them to me."

"Advance men, assistants," said Brad. "That has to cost money. Who pays them?"

"Donations from people like you and me. And Mr. Moody has a number of wealthy benefactors that help him spread the word of the Lord." As he continued to explain, it was clear that Reverend Wesley admired Dwight Moody.

"Then Mr. Moody evangelizes to bring people to the Lord, not to raise money or feel important," surmised Audrey.

"That's it in a nutshell," affirmed the reverend. "Now there are others, fakers, who act like evangelists, going from town to town, to talk folks into giving large donations. Some folks may be so taken that they give the fake preacher their life's savings, expecting him work miracles. After he collects a sizeable sum of money, he goes to a large city, such as San Francisco, Chicago, or New York and lives like a king."

"Your friend in Denver," asked Brad. "When do you think he'll tell you about Dr. Chetham?"

"I might have an answer as early as Monday."

"We'll be back Monday," said Audrey. "We've got to hurry, or we'll be late for dinner."

"We'll see you Sunday," said Mrs. Wesley.

"Good-bye," said Brad, as he and his sister scampered down the front steps.

"So," concluded Audrey as they hurried home, "a fake evangelist seeks donations. It's another kind of theft."

"Right," said Brad. "And the victims may never know that they were robbed. They believe they were helping people."

Audrey looked at her brother as they reached the outskirts of Riverton, and said, "Some place in the New Testament, Jesus warned about false prophets."

"Maybe we'll find out Monday," said Brad. "And if we find out that he is a fake," Brad paused, and looking at their house in the distance.

"If we find out that he is a fake, I know we'll think of something," finished Audrey.

"We've got plenty to do tomorrow," said Brad as they turned down the lane to their house. "First thing in the morning, we go to the Bar-X Ranch to help Hank Lacy."

As they approached the corral, Blaze and Ebony trotted out to meet them. Ebony bobbed her head and nickered as Brad reached out to pat her. Blaze hung her head over the fence and nuzzled Audrey.

"I'll bring both of you a carrot," said Brad, as he and Audrey headed to the house.

Brad opened the door and inhaled a delicious new aroma. "Nana, what are you cooking? It smells marvelous and I'm starving."

"You won't have to wait long," replied his grandmother. "It's fish from Vasya Petrov. I have plenty of wood, so just wash up for supper."

"What are you cooking with it, Nana?" asked Audrey.

"The usual: carrots, onions, potatoes, and baked apples."

Brad and Audrey quickly washed up and began setting the table. They had just finished when the front door opened.

"Victoria," said their father. "It smells wonderful. What is it?"

"It's fish. Vasya brought me some trout today. He went fishing and caught quite a few. He's still overwhelmed with the house that everyone built for him. I paid him for the fish and gave him a nice kosher lunch: coffee, apple pie, and a cheese sandwich."

"Kosher lunch," Brad wondered aloud, watching his father hang up his hat and coat. "What was kosher about it? And what does kosher mean?"

"To keep the Jewish faith," explained their grandmother, "there are certain foods that they don't eat, such as shellfish, and pork. In addition, they don't have milk and meat in the same meal."

"Then he would have had his coffee black if there was meat in the meal?" asked Audrey, placing a bowl of roasted vegetables on the table.

"That is correct," confirmed her grandmother,

placing the platter of fish in front of Harold. "But since there was no meat, he had milk in his coffee."

"How do you know this?" asked Brad.

"I lived in New York City," she explained. "I knew many Jewish people, had dinner with them, and learned about their faith."

"She was being a good neighbor, and a good Christian," added their mother, as everyone took a seat.

As the Bentons bowed their heads, Harold Benton thanked the Lord for the meal before them. Picking up the spatula, he put a large piece of fish on each of the plates that their mother held for him. When everyone had been served, they began eating.

"What did the reverend say?" asked their father looking at Brad and Audrey.

"He's sending a telegram to a friend in Denver," replied Brad. "He might have a reply by Monday."

Brad and Audrey related the rest of their conversation with Reverend Wesley about fake evangelists and Dwight Moody, carefully explaining that Dwight Moody was not a fake evangelist.

"The reverend said that Moody was a very successful businessman before he began his evangelizing," Audrey shared.

"And," said Brad, "he doesn't keep any of the money he receives from his book sales. All of his living expenses and the cost of his evangelical tours are paid by benefactors."

"All donations and book profits are given to a group of businessmen who manage the money and give it to Christian organizations," said Audrey.

"When President Lincoln called for 75,000

volunteers, some of the first volunteers were teachers and students from Moody's Sunday School classes," added their father.

"Cyrus McCormick and Lord Kinnaird are a couple of his benefactors," said Nana.

"McCormick, the farm equipment manufacturer?" asked Brad.

"Kinnaird, owner of the shipping line?" questioned Audrey.

"That's right," replied their mother. "Those men, and others such as Gustavus Swift, the owner of Swift and Company, pay for his tours."

"They provide him with the funds he needs for living expenses," explained their father. "That way all of the donations at his meetings go directly to the Church or Christian organizations."

"Father O'Brien told us that Reverend Moody presents the Bible in simple terms," said Brad.

"That's right," confirmed Nana. "I heard him in New York, and he preaches a very short sermon that's easy to understand. That's why he's so successful."

"Reverend Wesley's sermons are easy to understand, too," said Audrey.

"That's why our church is full each Sunday," explained their mother.

"That's why we're fortunate to have him as our Reverend," said Nana.

The discussion continued for almost an hour before Harold Benton looked at his pocket watch and said that it was getting late. Nana helped Audrey clear the table while Brad got the dishpan ready.

"I promised Blaze and Ebony carrots," said Brad, putting the last plate away. "Want to join me?"

"Of course," Audrey said, putting on her coat. "Let's go."

Brad put on his coat and picked up the two large carrots from the kitchen counter he had brought up from the cellar earlier. Audrey opened the door, and they headed for the corral. The sun had just set but they had no trouble seeing their horses waiting for them.

"Here's your carrot, Ebony," said Brad, offering the orange-colored root to his horse.

Audrey patted Blaze's neck as she held out the carrot. "Tomorrow we go to the Bar-X," said Audrey. "I want you to be strong and fast. We have to win the race against Ebony and Brad."

"You're challenging us to a race tomorrow?" There was a hint of excitement in his voice.

"How about from the edge of Riverton to the Bar-X?"

"Agreed," said Brad. "But the horses will expect one from the corral to the road, too."

"Fine," said Audrey. "And when we reach the Bar-X trail, they can cool down on the way to the ranch house."

"And the winner?"

"And the winner," said Audrey. "I don't know yet, but I'll think of something. Do you have any ideas?"

"I'll let you know by the time we start the race," said Brad. "Let's finish up and get to bed. Tomorrow will be more demanding than sitting in a classroom."

CHAPTER 5

Saturday morning, 18 April 1881: "Thanks for breakfast, Nana," said Brad. "I'll get you some more wood before we leave for the Bar-X."

"Now none of that Pinkerton stuff, you hear?" chided their grandmother, a twinkle in her eye.

"Why, Nana," Audrey piously replied, "We won't be doing any Pinkertoning until Reverend Wesley receives a reply to his telegram."

"And that will be Monday, at the earliest," added Brad, trying to sound innocent like his sister.

"I feel better already," said their mother, dramatically placing the back of her hand against her forehead and looking at the ceiling. "Let Reverend Wesley and Father O'Brien handle this Dr. Chetham."

"If this keeps up we can open a theater. The Benton Players, Riverton's own theater group," declared their father.

"We'll be at the Bar-X," said Brad, becoming serious. "Besides, Dr. Jeremiah Chetham doesn't arrive until next Saturday."

"The two of you stay with Hank Lacy," instructed their father. "He needs your help checking out the old Big Foot Ranch. He wants to use it as a northern line shack for his men."

36

"The Bar-X does have quite a bit more range to cover since they bought the Big Foot Ranch," said Brad.

"Would you like to ride to town with us, Pa?" asked Audrey.

"I think I would," he said, stirring some milk into his coffee.

"I'll get the horses ready," volunteered Brad, grabbing three small apples as he left.

Blaze and Ebony came to the tack room door to be saddled as Brad entered the barn. He gave Ebony an apple, put on her saddle blanket, and then her saddle. After tightening the cinch, he did the same for Blaze. As he was finishing, Audrey, arrived and started putting on the bridles.

"Ginger is learning how get an apple; she comes to be saddled," said Brad, giving his father's horse an apple.

"Your apple method works very well," Audrey confirmed, watching her brother saddle the horse.

Audrey opened the corral gate and Brad led the three horses out. When he reached the hitching rail, he looped their reins over it. Looking expectantly at the house, he saw their father come out, put on his hat, and head toward them.

"Let's mount up," said their father, putting his foot into the stirrup and swinging his leg over the saddle. As soon as Brad and Audrey were mounted, he clucked and gently nudged his horse to a comfortable trot. The horses quickly aligned themselves three abreast as they rode down the lane. They reached the stage office in just a few minutes.

"Say hello to Hank for me," said their father, dismounting.

"Bye, Pa!" said Audrey.

"See you tonight!" called Brad, as he and his sister walked their horses down Main Street.

"Still think you can win a race to the Bar-X?" challenged Brad, as they passed the last building on Main Street.

"I gave Blaze an extra carrot this morning," said Audrey, suppressing a smile. "That will give her the extra stamina she needs to win."

Brad looked at his sister, not believing what he had heard. "An extra carrot!" he exclaimed, just before he saw the smile spread across her face.

"Ready for the race?" said Audrey gently reining Blaze to a stop.

"If I win," said Brad, shaking his head, "you have to stop tricking me for, uh, a month."

"Agreed," said Audrey, her eyes twinkling over a big smile. "And if I win, the next time Wilma Sue is over, you act like an English butler and serve us tea and cookies."

"You want me to be an English butler for you and Wilma Sue for an afternoon?" said Brad. "Where did you dream that up?"

"The first morning we were out searching for Pa, you had a mug of hot tea ready for me when you woke me up. It was marvelous, and I've never forgotten it."

Brad looked at his sister; her face was sober, without a hint of a smile or smirk.

"You're serious," he said. "You're really serious."

"Yes, I'm serious."

"Fine, but I'd do that for you and Wilma Sue even if I win the race."

"The count of three," said Audrey, the mischievous glint once again in her eyes.

"One," said Brad, leaning forward in his saddle. The horses tensed and prepared to race. "Two, three!" he shouted.

The horses broke into an immediate gallop, side by side, racing toward the Bar-X. The warm air from their nostrils created clouds of steam in the cool morning air as they galloped down the road.

"There's the trail," yelled Brad later. "The first one to pass under the sign wins."

"Come on, Blaze," begged Audrey, leaning low and patting her horse's neck. "Please!" Blaze slowly pulled ahead, passing under the sign half a length ahead of Ebony.

"English butler service will be available later this week," conceded Brad, as the horses settled into a slow trot.

"There's the ranch," said Audrey, as they topped the crest of a gentle hill. Brad gently reined Ebony to a walk to cool down after their race.

Stopping at the hitching rail, they dismounted and headed toward the bunkhouse where the foreman, Hank Lacy, was talking to his men. Mr. Lacy briefly put up his hand, asking them to wait a moment. As the ranch hands headed to the corral and their horses, Brad and Audrey walked up to him.

"Morning, Mr. Lacy," said Brad.

"Morning, Brad, Audrey," he replied, as they headed toward the corral. "We'll be going to the Big Foot Ranch to check it out and make a list of needed supplies."

"Should I have Cookie hold lunch for you, Mr. Lacy?" asked Zeke, one of the ranch hands.

"No," he replied, mounting his horse. "We'll be back by noon, and we'll be hungry."

The ranch foreman gently prodded his horse into a fast trot and Brad and Audrey fell in behind him. They headed west toward the main road, then turned north toward the Big Foot Mine. As they reached the trail to the Big Foot Ranch, they slowed the horses to a walk.

"What's at the ranch?" asked Audrey.

"Not much," replied Hank, "the main house, a small bunk house, barn, and the corral."

"That would make a real nice line-shack," said Brad.

"That's what we want," Hank confirmed. "The men can check the cattle in that area and have a nice place to stay, especially in bad weather."

"How long will it take to get there?" asked Audrey.

"About half an hour more, I expect," said Hank, looking at the hills to the east. "We're on good horses and a clear road. The cowboys would be on tired horses and going through brush, and rough terrain. It would take them longer to travel back to the Bar-X. When they're in the north range, this can save the men two to three hours a day of traveling to and from the Bar-X."

"There's the cut-off," said Brad, pointing to a trail ahead and to their right.

"We'll be there shortly," said Hank. He studied the sky a moment before continuing, "It's going to be a nice day. The sky is clear, no wind."

"That is just we need after a hard winter," said Audrey.

Brad reined Ebony to the right as they headed

down the trail to Big Foot Ranch. The trail was a little overgrown with grass and weeds from lack of use.

"Looks like some of your men have been out here recently," said Brad. "The grass has been knocked down by a horse."

"Looks like it," agreed Hank. "There's the ranch house. Let's tie up out front."

Audrey dismounted and tied Blaze to the hitching rail. Hank and Brad did the same, each wrapping the reins over the rail.

"I've got the paper and pencil, Mr. Lacy," said Audrey pulling a pad out of her saddlebag.

"We'll start with the ranch house, then the bunk house and barn," explained Hank, starting up the short walkway.

"I'll get the door," said Brad, taking a few long strides to reach the door first.

They entered the house and stopped a moment to let their eyes adjust from the bright sunlight. Straight ahead of them was a large stone fireplace. A number of chairs and a large table were at the side of the room next to the kitchen.

"Reach for the clouds and don't turn around," ordered a man behind them. Audrey gasped, then Hank, Brad, and Audrey slowly raised their hands as ordered. "Unbuckle your gun belt, slowly, let it drop to the floor."

"I don't have much money, mister, but you're welcome to it," said Mr. Lacy.

"Don't talk," growled the man. "Just do what I tell you to do. You two men take three steps forward, then lie face down on the floor, and put your hands behind your heads. The girl stays where she is."

Hank and Brad did as ordered. They heard the man pull Hank's gun belt across the floor.

"Now, young lady, please put your hands behind your back."

The man quickly tied Audrey's hands with some rawhide strips, sat her on the floor, and tied her feet together.

"Now, young man, stand up, but keep facing the fireplace, and slowly back up until you're beside the young lady. Now, move her to the fireplace." Brad did so, propping Audrey up against its stone face.

"Good! Now, put your hands behind you and back up slowly. Don't try anything or this pistol can be a painful experience."

"Yes, sir," said Brad, placing his hands behind him and backing up to the man. In a minute, Brad's hands were tied behind his back, he was pushed to the floor, and his feet were tied.

'You're next, mister," commanded the man. "Do the same as your young friend."

Hank stood up, placed his hands behind him, and slowly backed up until he was told to stop. When the man finished, he pulled Hank and Brad to the fireplace, propping them up beside Audrey.

Brad studied the man, looking for something unusual, an identifying scar, or distinctive clothing. He was about five feet ten inches in height and of slender build. His hat covered most of his dark hair. A mask covered his face, except for two small holes for his eyes. The man took a rope and tied all of their feet together.

When he finished, he emptied Hank's pockets, and then Brad's pockets, stuffing the money in his jacket.

"Young lady, do you have any money in your pockets?"

"I have about fifty cents," answered Audrey, boldly.

"Rather than search a lady, I'll take you at your word and leave you with your money. Good day," he said, as he left the house and closed the door.

Audrey gave a sigh of relief; Brad and Mr. Lacy started breathing normally again.

They heard him go down the steps. A few minutes later the hoof beats of his horse gradually faded away.

"That was quite a welcome to the Big Foot Ranch," observed Hank.

"This place must attract outlaws," replied Audrey. "First the Big Foot Gang, and now this."

"Don't forget that Uncle Henry used this as his headquarters when he started his search for Duke Badger," said Brad.

"I'm going to rub these rawhide strips against the fireplace stones," said Hank. "You two do the same."

About an hour later, Brad said, "It's no use, the stones are too smooth."

"Same here," said Hank. "What about you, Audrey?"

"I've been rubbing on the mortar," said Audrey. "One of the strips is now free. And, I'm cold," she said with exasperation.

"If we're not home by supper time, Pa will come looking for us," said Brad.

Another hour passed, and though futile, they continued rubbing the rawhide against the rocks and mortar. The early afternoon sun came through the windows, warming the house and reflecting off of the dust and cobwebs hanging from the rafters.

"I'm hungry," declared Brad.

"You're always hungry," replied his sister. "If we're lucky, we'll have a late supper tonight."

"Or maybe breakfast tomorrow morning," sighed Hank.

"Uh," said Brad hesitantly, "I, uh, have to go to the privy."

"Well," laughed Hank, "that does present a little problem, doesn't it?"

"It certainly does," lamented Brad.

"You'll just have to go in your pants," declared Audrey. "Pa said men did in the Civil war. Sometimes the enemy's fire was so intense that they couldn't go to the bushes, or even move."

"Don't talk or think about it," suggested Hank. "That only makes the need greater."

"Any idea who that man was?" asked Audrey, changing the subject.

"No," answered Brad. "But there was something familiar about his voice."

"What was it?" asked Hank.

"I haven't been able to place it," said Brad. "But his voice was familiar."

"Hopefully it will come to you," suggested Hank. "You'll probably wake up in the middle of the night with the answer."

"Was he a member of the Big Foot Gang?" asked Audrey.

"No, but his voice sounded familiar, and his breath smelled of whiskey."

"It did," said Audrey. "And, he was polite. He was very gentle when he tied my hands. He even helped me down to the floor so he could tie my feet."

"Same here," said Brad. "He wasn't rough, but he wasn't gentle, either."

"You're not a woman, either" replied Hank. "But it does appear that we were robbed by a very well-mannered outlaw."

"Quiet," whispered Brad. "I think I hear a horse coming."

"I hear it too," whispered Audrey. "I hope he's not coming back."

"We'll soon find out," replied Hank.

CHAPTER 6

The three listened intently as the rider stopped in front of the ranch house. The creak of saddle leather could be heard over the afternoon serenade of the birds. The rider dismounted, and they could hear his spurs jingle as he came up the front walk. He stopped on the front porch for what seemed like an eternity before grasping and turning the doorknob.

"Mr. Lacy, Brad, Audrey!" exclaimed Zeke, standing in the doorway, looking at the trio in front of the fireplace. "What happened?"

"Someone was here when we arrived," explained Hank, as Zeke cut the rawhide strips. "As soon as we entered the house, he told us to reach for the clouds."

"He took Mr. Lacy's gun belt, tied us up, took our money, and left," recounted Brad, leaning forward so Zeke could cut his hands free.

"Other than being cold and hungry, we're fine," complained Audrey, rubbing her wrists.

"Excuse me," muttered Brad. "I have to go to the privy. I'll be right back."

"I'm coming, too," said Audrey, following her brother out the door.

"I think all of us have to go, Zeke," said Hank looking

46

at the sun. "We've been tied up for about, uh, since we arrived."

"Cookie and I decided about one o'clock that I should come check on you," said Zeke. "It's about three quarters of an hour's ride from the Bar-X."

"We've been tied up for about five hours," surmised Hank. "We left the Bar-X after eight this morning and got here about nine."

"Mr. Lacy," said Brad. "The outlaw took your rifle from your horse, too."

"We'd better check the kitchen, bunkhouse, and barn to see what else is missing," sighed Hank resignedly. "Zeke, you and Brad check the barn; make a list of what was taken and what we might need. Audrey and I will check the ranch house and do the same. We'll meet in the bunkhouse when we're done."

A quarter of an hour later, the four of them met in the bunkhouse. Audrey had a sheet of paper listing the missing and needed items, as did Brad.

"Well," concluded Hank. "It looks like small, easy to sell items were taken: my pistol and rifle, an axe, two shovels, and some kitchen items - and, of course, our money."

"He took things that could be easily carried on a horse or in a saddlebag," said Brad, thoughtfully.

"They were the same kind of items that were stolen from our house," said Audrey.

"Your Pa told me about that," said Hank, "Brad's rifle, your Ma's gold locket, a cooking pot, and a pie, if I recall correctly."

"Well, he took a loaf of bread, too," said Brad. "And our skillet."

"We've got what we came out for," said Hank. "Let's go back to the Bar-X. Hopefully Cookie saved some lunch for us."

"The men were coming back for seconds," recalled Zeke as he mounted his horse. "Cookie had made chili and cornbread, one of their favorites."

"Now my stomach is growling," lamented Brad. "Chili and cornbread is one of my favorites, too."

"We've got to keep the horses moving," giggled Audrey, "otherwise Brad may eat their hooves."

"I can practically smell Cookie's chili already," Hank lamented, as they reined their horses away from the hitching rail. "Move out!"

The horses gracefully loped along the trail as they rode away from the Big Foot Ranch.

"More cornbread, Brad?" offered Cookie.

"Please, and thanks for making another batch."

"Zeke and I knew something wasn't right when you weren't back by noon," said Cookie. "I expected the three of you around noon. At one o'clock, Zeke saddled up and headed for the Big Foot."

"I kept a lookout for your horses," said Zeke. "As I was riding I couldn't help but think that maybe a grizzly, or even Big Foot, had spooked the horses, leaving all of you without mounts."

"I would have thought the same thing," said Hank, picking up his mug of coffee. "An outlaw tying us up and taking our valuables would never have crossed my mind."

"Robbers go for trains, stagecoaches, and banks,"

said Cookie, ladling more chili onto Hank and Brad's plates."

"That's right," said Zeke. "I ought to know. I helped rob the stage last year."

"That's behind you now," counseled Hank gently.

"Yes," said Audrey. "Keep the faith and do what is right. I don't want you going back to prison."

"Or getting shot during a holdup," added Brad.

"Reverend Wesley helped me see that I'd gone wrong," said Zeke. "I promised the reverend that I'd stop taking things that weren't mine. I can never go back to robbing."

"When the reverend told me about you finding the Lord, that's when I knew I wanted you at the Bar-X," said Hank. "This is your home until you decide to move on."

"Speaking about moving on," said Brad. "We should be heading home. Sheriff Tate is on the way, so we'll tell him about the robbery."

"Good," said Hank. "I'll see him tomorrow in case he has any more questions."

"Buckley Hodges is watching out for my rifle," said Brad, pushing his chair back. "You might want to give him the description and serial numbers of your pistol and rifle, too."

"I'll do that at church tomorrow," replied Hank.

"We'll see you tomorrow, then," said Audrey, putting on her coat. Brad and Audrey mounted their horses and clucked them into an easy lope.

After a while, Audrey broke the silence. "I think the man who robbed us this morning is the same man who robbed our house. What do you think?"

"I'm inclined to agree with you. It's also possible that there is a gang robbing empty homes. The robber, or robbers, haven't held up a store, or robbed a house with people in it."

"True," said Audrey. "The Big Foot Ranch was empty until we arrived this morning."

Brad and Audrey looped their reins over the hitching rail in front of the sheriff's office.

"That's pretty much what happened, Sheriff," said Brad. "As soon as we entered the ranch house, we were told to reach for the clouds."

"He had a bandana covering his entire face, except for two eye holes," added Audrey.

"I want you two to keep quiet about this," ordered the sheriff. "There have been a number of small burglaries the past week. No one's been hurt yet, and I want to keep it that way. The two of you, and Hank Lacy, are the first folks to actually see the robber."

"Or at least one of the robbers," countered Audrey.

"True," conceded the sheriff. "You've seen a robber. I know I can trust you two Pinkertons, so keep your eyes and ears open. Don't say anything about the fact that the robber's voice sounded familiar. If he thinks you're on to him, your lives could be in danger. I'll tell Hank to keep quiet about it too when I see him tomorrow morning."

"We've got to tell Pa," insisted Audrey.

"That goes without saying, but no one else, except your Ma and Victoria. And be sure to tell them to keep it quiet as well."

"We will," agreed Brad, opening the door to leave.

"I know you two pretty well," said Sheriff Tate. "I also know you'll be cooking up some kind of plan."

Brad grinned, and Audrey's face flushed as she looked Sheriff Tate straight in the eye and said, "Yes, I have been thinking of a plan. After I talk it over with Brad and Nana, I'll let you know what it is."

"Fair enough," replied the sheriff. "Now hustle on to your Pa. I don't want you to miss him; he'll be heading home in a bit."

They mounted their horses and started toward the stage office when Brad stopped and said, "Let's stop and talk to Reverend Wesley first."

"Yes," said Audrey, as they turned their horses around. "We can tell him and still make it to the stage office before five o'clock."

"I find your story very intriguing," concluded Reverend Wesley, looking thoughtfully at Brad and Audrey. "What have you got to say about it, Trevor?"

Father O'Brien smiled as he rubbed his chin. "I believe this puzzle will start coming together when we get a response from your friend in Denver. I talked with Sheriff Tate earlier today. He, too, is concerned about the burglaries the past few weeks. I'm sure that these burglaries, your experience this morning, and Dr. Jeremiah Chetham, are related."

"Can we meet again Monday morning?" asked Reverend Wesley. "Say about ten o'clock?"

Brad looked at Audrey, who nodded agreement. "Yes," he said, "We can meet then."

"We've got to hurry to the stage office right now," said Audrey. "Pa's expecting us by five."

"Don't let me keep you," replied the reverend, standing up.

"See you tomorrow," said Father O'Brien. "I'll be helping Bob at his service."

Brad and Audrey quickly mounted their horses and clucked them to a fast walk. When they reached the stage office, their father was locking the door.

"Perfect timing," he said. "You can tell me about your day as we ride home."

"We have a lot to tell you," cautioned Brad as his father mounted his horse.

"The way you said that makes me nervous. Is something wrong?"

'Yes, Pa," said Audrey as they started down the street. "Brad and I will be Pinkertons for a while."

"I see," acknowledged their father. "Should I wait until dinner so your ma and Victoria can hear too?"

"I think that would be best," said Brad.

"Hank Lacy, Brad, and I were tied up and robbed this morning," blurted Audrey. "No one was hurt. We'll tell you the rest at dinner."

Their father opened his mouth, then closed it. Nodded thoughtfully and said, "Now I know why you said you'll be Pinkertons for a while," chuckled their father, urging his horse to a fast trot.

"Amen," said their father.

"Okay," admonished Nana, as their mother held the first plate for her husband. "We've waited long enough. You young Pinkertons must tell us what happened today."

"We went to the Bar-X and met Mr. Lacy," said Audrey as her father put a slice of roast venison on a plate. "He wanted to check out the Big Foot Ranch."

Brad and Audrey continued, and by the time they had finished supper, their parents and Victoria had heard the whole story, including the well-known Bar-X cornbread and chili.

"So," concluded their mother, "you think all these new folks with ailments, the evangelistic healer, and the robberies are connected."

"Yes," said Audrey, "we do."

"I don't know about that," replied their father, "but I did talk to Buckley Hodges about a small pistol for your mother. He also suggested a small shotgun for Victoria."

"What about your shotgun?" asked Audrey.

"Mine is too big and heavy for her. He recommended a .20-gauge shotgun. It has a lot less kick than my .12-gauge."

"Any robber that comes while I'm here will be sorry," pronounced Nana. "He'll either be seeing Doc Adams to get patched up or Reverend Wesley will be conducting his funeral."

Brad and Audrey looked at their grandmother, their mouths open in disbelief.

"Don't be shocked by what I said. I know how to use a gun. A robber that comes into this house while I'm here is up to no good. I've had friends killed by burglars, and I don't intend to be like them. It it's me or the burglar, I'm going to make it the burglar."

Abby Benton looked at her children and said, "When

you were in that cave hiding from Duke Badger, if he'd come in for you or had started shooting, you would have shot back, wouldn't you?"

"Well, yes," said Brad. "But I didn't want to."

"I know you didn't," said their grandmother. "But if he and his partner had come into the cave with their guns drawn..."

"We would have shot them," said Brad very softly. "I had chambered a shell into my rifle, cocked the hammer, and had it pointing at them."

"It was a 'you or them' situation," Nana said matter-of-factly. "You would have shot them, if necessary."

"I understand," whispered Audrey.

"So do I," said Brad. "You have to defend yourself."

"First thing Monday, Brad and I are meeting with Reverend Wesley and Father O'Brien," said Audrey.

"The reverend should have an answer to the wire he sent his friend in Denver," added Brad.

"I'll be staying home from church tomorrow," declared Nana. "Reverend Wesley and I talked about it a few days ago when he stopped by. Your Pa is leaving his pistol with me."

"It's getting late," noted their father. "Let's clean up, lock the doors, and go to bed."

"Right, Pa," said Brad. "It has been a long day and I'm tired."

"Me too," said Audrey.

Brad and Audrey cleared the table, did the dishes, said good night to their parents, and headed up the stairs. But instead of going to bed, they slipped into Brad's room, closed the door, and assumed their usual place, with Audrey on the floor beside the chest of drawers and Brad leaning against the bed, his hands behind his head.

"I finally placed the man's voice," said Brad. "Franz Hall, the man with the bad leg."

"But the outlaw didn't limp at all," countered Audrey. "Franz Hall has a bad leg."

"I know, but I'm sure of it."

"Maybe Father O'Brien can help," said Audrey. "He said he thought Monday's wire would help bring the pieces of the puzzle together."

"We'll know Monday," said Brad. "You don't think I'm crazy, do you?"

"No, I don't think you're crazy. Their voices are similar, and I did smell whiskey on Mr. Hall's breath at church last week. And he also called me a young lady."

"Let's go to bed," said Brad.

"Tomorrow, Buck's Pa is supposed to bring the pistols and shotgun to church," said Audrey.

"Nana is right," said Brad, standing up. "But I hope a robber doesn't come. I don't want her to have to shoot someone."

"Neither do I," said Audrey, as she left the room. "Neither do I."

CHAPTER 7

Palm Sunday, 11 April 1881: "Thanks for the early breakfast, Nana," said Audrey. "We want to talk to Reverend Wesley before church this morning."

Brad came through the back door and said "Pa, I've hitched your horse to the buggy. It's tied to the hitching rail."

"Thanks, son, your Ma and I will see you at church."

"Bye, Pa, Ma," said Audrey.

They left the house and headed to the corral. "Do you still think Franz Hall was the robber yesterday?" asked Audrey.

"I'm not sure enough to testify in court," answered Brad. "But I'm sure enough to look for more evidence to prove, or disprove, my belief."

"A race to the road?" challenged Audrey, mounting Blaze.

"Fine, maybe I'll win today," said Brad, reining Ebony away from the corral. "On the count of three: One! Two! Three!"

The horses bolted to a gallop for their ritual race to the road. Ebony lengthened her stride and reached the road a neck ahead of Blaze.

The horses settled into a slow trot as they headed

to Riverton. "What's that in the road?" asked Audrey, pointing to a frost-covered object.

"It looks like a gun belt," suggested Brad, dismounting. He picked up the bundle of leather and said, "It is, with a Colt Peacemaker pistol, like Pa's."

"Let's take it to Sheriff Tate," said Audrey. "With all the robberies, someone has probably reported it stolen."

"Or they will report it stolen," replied Brad, looping the gun belt across his saddle horn.

"Sheriff Tate is usually in his office by nine," said Audrey, clucking Blaze to a fast trot.

"Even on Sunday," noted Brad, as Ebony matched her gait with Blaze.

Upon entering Riverton, they slowed their horses to a walk. After passing the general store, they reined their horses to the sheriff's office hitching rail.

"I can smell the coffee," said Brad. "He must be in."

"Back so soon?" greeted the sheriff as they entered.

"We found this gun belt in the road," said Brad, handing it to the sheriff. "With all the robberies, we thought it may have been reported stolen."

"Or someone will report it stolen," predicted Audrey.

"Where did you find it, specifically?" asked the sheriff.

"About 30 yards from the lane to our house," Audrey explained. "It was wrapped up and covered with frost."

"I'll check my list of stolen property and see if it's been reported. And I'd appreciate it if you didn't tell anyone about finding it. I want to keep the robber guessing. And let me know if you see anyone in your area riding down the road looking for something. Don't talk to them; just say hello and keep going. Then, the next time you see me, tell me who they were."

"We will," agreed Audrey. "We've got to go now. We want to talk to Reverend Wesley before church."

"I'll see you shortly," said the sheriff. "I'm picking up your teacher, Miss Jones, in a little bit."

When they reached the church, the Catholic service had just finished, and Father O'Brien was saying good-bye to the last few members of his congregation. Reverend Wesley had left his house, but was still a half-block away.

"Looks like we arrived at just the right time," observed Brad.

"It certainly looks that way," said his sister as she waved to the reverend.

"Good morning, Brad, Audrey," greeted Father O'Brien.

"Morning, Father," replied Brad.

"How are the Pinkertons this fine Palm Sunday?" he asked.

"How do you do it?" giggled Audrey. "You read my mind, just like Mr. Acker."

"It's a special gift possessed by priests and rabbis," replied Father O'Brien with a twinkle in his eye. Then as Reverend Wesley joined them, he added, "Some reverends have that ability, too. Isn't that right, Bob?"

"Whatever you say," said the reverend. "What can we do for our Pinkertons this morning?"

Father O'Brien laughed and Audrey blushed at the reverend's question. Reverend Wesley gave Father O'Brien a puzzled look, and Brad raised his hands in futility.

"I asked Father O'Brien how he knew why we were here," said Audrey. "And he said that it is a special gift of priests and reverends. And..."

Before Audrey could say anything else, Reverend Wesley said, "Trevor is right. It is a special gift. But since we only have a few minutes before people start arriving, tell us what you have come up with about the robberies."

"I realized last night that the robber at the Big Foot Ranch was Franz Hall," answered Brad. "Or at least he certainly sounded like Franz Hall."

"And, the robber's breath smelled of whiskey, just like Franz Hall's breath did last week," said Audrey.

Reverend Wesley and Father O'Brien gave each other a knowing look and nodded to one another. Audrey looked at them questioningly, feeling as though she had come in at the end of a conversation.

"I think the puzzle is coming together," said Father O'Brien, nodding toward the Hodges' buckboard turning off the street to the back of the church. "We can discuss this further Monday morning. Bob's congregation is starting to arrive."

"Let's go see the guns that Mr. Hodges brought," suggested Brad.

"I see Ma and Pa coming," said Audrey. "We might as well wait for them."

Harold Benton parked the buggy beside the Hodges' buckboard and climbed down. Brad helped his mother down while his father and Mr. Hodges un-wrapped the shotgun.

"It's light and doesn't have much kick," said Mr. Hodges. "This .20-gauge has a lot less kick than your Pa's .12-gauge."

Brad picked up the open shotgun, assured that it was not loaded, and then handed it to his mother. Abby took it from her son, lifted it up and down to feel the weight, and then handed to Audrey who did the same.

"What about the pistols?" asked Harold.

Mr. Hodges reached inside his jacket and handed one to Mr. Benton. "It's a .32 caliber," he said. "Light, small, and it fits a woman's hand better than the .44 or .45. It has less kick, too."

Mr. Hodges opened the cylinder to assure that it was unloaded, and then handed it to Mrs. Benton. She took it with her right hand, transferred it to her left hand, and then back to her right hand.

"It is light," she agreed, "and it's easier to grip than Harold's pistol."

"The .38 is quite a bit heavier," said Mr. Hodges. "The .32 is really ideal for a woman. A man uses his pistol to shoot snakes, for close up defense from critters when he's on the open range. If Abby or Victoria were herding cattle, I'd encourage them to use a bigger caliber, at least a .38. Since they're using it for personal defense, in the home, the .32 is lighter, and it can be carried rather easily in the pocket of a skirt or dress. The relatively light weight and smaller size of the .32 also allows it to be carried in a woman's purse and still leave room for her personal items. The next choice, which I don't recommend, would be a derringer."

"Why don't you recommend a derringer?"

"One shot, or two, depending on the model," he said. "That is all. The .32 is more versatile and it has six shots, five if you leave one chamber empty. If you wish, I can get a small shoulder holster that you could wear under a jacket. I recommend that you get two of the .32-caliber pistols."

"Buck, I mean Buckley," said Mrs. Benton, "Victoria and I are not gunfighters, but I like your recommendation. We'll take two of the .32 caliber pistols and carry them in a pocket or a purse."

"Good," he said. "I'll load them now, leaving the chamber under the hammer empty; that prevents an accidental discharge if you drop it. You can put yours in your purse now, and Harold can put Victoria's in his pocket. I'll put the rest of the box of ammunition under the seat of your buggy."

"We'll take the shotgun, too," decided Harold. "And put a box of shells with the .32 ammunition. I'll rewrap the shotgun and put it behind the piano during the service. With the thieving that's going on, I certainly don't want to leave it in the buggy."

"And time has flown," said Abby. "I've got to get ready for the service. Thank you so much, Buckley. I do appreciate your concern and recommendations."

They went into the church, Harold carrying the shotgun wrapped in its cloth bag. Brad and Audrey stayed outside, talking with Buck while they waited for Wilma Sue.

"Pa's sold pistols to other folks, too," said Buck. "Everyone has had something stolen. No one has been robbed at gunpoint yet, and no one has seen one of the burglars."

Brad looked at Audrey knowingly, then back at Buck. "Has anyone tried to sell a used gun to your Pa?"

"Not yet," he replied. "Pa thinks they won't even try. He expects that they'll go to another town, like Denver, Santa Fe, or St. Louis. Experienced thieves know that Pa would recognize the guns that he's sold or worked on."

"The Bevinses are here," said Brad, watching an approaching buggy.

"Wilma Sue may have heard something about other burglaries," said Buck.

"I think she has," said Audrey. "She's waving her index finger, not her whole hand."

"I don't understand." questioned Buck.

"When Wilma Sue waves her whole hand, she is saying hello. If she waves her index finger, she is saying 'wait a moment, I have something to say.'"

"Oh," said Buck, nodding slowly.

"I'll be right in, Ma," said Wilma Sue as she walked towards them.

"What have you heard?" asked Audrey.

"Almost all of our customers are talking about the burglaries."

"Do you have any suspicions?" questioned Audrey.

"No, all our customers have been polite, and that includes the people new to Riverton."

"Ma is playing the prelude," said Brad. "We'd better go in."

Brad and Audrey slipped in beside their father before their mother finished the prelude. There was a moment of silence as Abby opened the hymnal. When she started playing the introduction to the opening hymn, the congregation stood up. As usual, Reverend Wesley sang enthusiastically as he strode down the aisle. The deacons read the scriptures for the day, and then the reverend began his sermon.

"Today, my sermon comes from Matthew, chapter 7, verse 15. Matthew quotes Jesus who warns the people to beware of false prophets. They may be dressed to look like sheep, but inside they are ferocious wolves. They claim, or they appear to claim, that they were sent by God, when they were not. Later in Chapter 24, verse 24, he warns that false prophets will come and perform miracles. Their miracles will deceive even the religious leaders."

Brad looked around the congregation and saw people wide-eyed, looking at each other. They knew that the reverend was referring to Dr. Jeremiah Chetham. Was he warning them because he thought Chetham was a fake or because he was afraid that Dr. Jeremiah Chetham might cure people's afflictions, turning them away from Reverend Wesley?

Brad leaned over and whispered into Audrey's ear, "I think Reverend Wesley has their attention."

Audrey waited a moment and then whispered into her brother's ear, "He hasn't called Dr. Chetham a fake, or a false prophet. He's just telling them that there are false prophets."

"I know," whispered Brad. "Maybe we'll find out tomorrow if Dr. Jeremiah Chetham is a false prophet."

Reverend Wesley knew he had the congregation's attention as he continued. "Jeremiah, chapter 23, verse 16, says the Lord Almighty warns us not to listen to these prophets. They speak visions from their own minds, not from the Lord. These false prophets live a lie; they strengthen the evildoers. They are like the people of Sodom and Gomorrah."

When it came time for announcements, Reverend Wesley walked down to the front pews and said, "I believe that everyone in this congregation knows about the recent spate of burglaries. Thankfully, no one has been hurt. Unfortunately, we have no idea who is committing these crimes. Sheriff Tate needs everyone's help. If you have any information, no matter how trivial, that can be linked to the burglaries, please let him know. I also know that everyone is fearful that they might be in their home when the burglar or burglars enter. People don't want to get hurt, so they're locking their doors at night and when they leave their homes."

There were nods of agreement, and folks murmured words of encouragement to each other. When the chatter died down, the reverend continued. "Be careful, don't let your fear cause you to shoot at sounds or to shoot your neighbors. Fear is one of Satan's allies. It is better to get robbed than to mistakenly kill your neighbor."

Again, there was a swell of talking, head-shaking, and head-nodding at the reverend's statement. Harold Benton gently grasped his daughter's hand; Audrey squeezed his in return.

"Now don't misunderstand me," continued the reverend. "Most of you know that I was a Deputy Sheriff at one time and that I still carry a pistol. If someone breaks into my home with evil intent, rest assured that it will be an unpleasant experience. Sheriff Tate may have a new boarder, Doc Adams may have a patient, or Father O'Brien and I will be conducting a graveside service. I expect every one of you to do the same."

The congregation was silent. They knew their pastor, a man of the cloth, was a fighter, and they were proud of him.

"Abby," said Reverend Wesley, "the offertory, please."

"Tell me about the sermon," said Nana as she poured herself a second cup of tea.

"He warned us about false prophets," said Brad, as he cut a piece of pie.

"And not to let fear control our lives," added Audrey. "He also said a burglar would have an unpleasant experience if they broke into his home while he was in it."

"He encouraged everyone to lock their doors at night and when they leave their house," said Harold Benton. "And I have a pistol for you, Victoria, a .32 caliber. It's light, it's made for a woman's hand."

"Harold, I want you to take me out to the creek and give me a review on how to use the pistol. Abby, you should come, too."

"I wouldn't miss it," vowed Nana's daughter, placing her hand assuringly on her husband's arm.

It was midafternoon when the Bentons assembled near the creek. Abby and Nana had their pistols, and Brad carried some extra shells in his jacket pocket. Audrey and Brad set up dozens of pinecones along the fence rail while their father reviewed gun safety with his wife and mother-in-law.

"I want everyone to stand behind the firing line," he ordered. "Victoria, I'll start with you. Grip the pistol as I've told you. That's right, cock the hammer with your thumb, aim, and gently squeeze the trigger."

Brad saw the pinecone disintegrate at the same time they heard the sound of the discharge. Nana aimed and squeezed the trigger again and again until all five shells had been fired.

"Very good!" congratulated Audrey. "You hit four of the pinecones. I didn't know you could shoot like that."

"My father, your great-grandfather, taught me how to shoot," Nana explained, smiling proudly. "Your father retaught me, and this .32 is a nice little pistol. And it is much lighter and easier to hold than his Peacemaker."

She put the .32 in her dress pocket, and Abby moved up beside her husband. "Your father taught me how to shoot after we were married." Looking at her children she continued, "but like your grandmother I haven't shot a pistol for years."

Abby followed her husband's instructions and shot five times, hitting three of the pinecones. "It is a nice little pistol," she said, turning it in her hand.

"If a real danger appears," he continued, "you probably won't consciously think about the process you just learned. But it is very important to know it and to remember that you have plenty of time to aim and to squeeze the trigger."

"It seems like forever," commented Audrey, "but it is only a second."

"Audrey is correct," confirmed her father. "If it is a burglar, he's probably going to be very close to you, probably in the same room. He'll be surprised when you pull a gun on him. Take immediate command of the situation. Don't let him start a conversation with you or move toward you. If he doesn't do exactly what you tell him to do or moves toward you, shoot him. If you hesitate, even for a moment, that may give him the time he needs to knock your gun away or draw his own gun and shoot you."

The Bentons started back to the house. The meaning

of what their father had just told them ran through their minds. Audrey was the first to speak.

"Pa," she said, as they approached the barn, "I was thinking about the man who tied us up yesterday. Mr. Lacy said he would have shot us if we hadn't obeyed him. Yet, he didn't use foul language and was polite while he robbed us."

"The robber wasn't expecting you," said her father, opening the back door. "You had trapped him. And Hank was right. If you hadn't obeyed the robber, he probably would have started shooting."

"I don't want those burglars to ruin my entire vacation," Audrey declared. "So, I'm going to start sewing my new dress and then I'm going to read a book."

"What are your plans, Brad?" asked his father.

"Harry Acker loaned me the English translation of *20,000 Leagues Under the Sea.* I want to read it." Brad paused for a moment, winked at his father, then looked at his sister. "And with Audrey's help, of course, catch the burglars."

"Brad Benton," she exclaimed. "I told you I wanted to sew a new dress!" Seeing her father's smile and Brad's pious look, she continued, "Brad Benton, you. . . you. . . exasperate me some times!"

"What time do you plan on seeing Reverend Wesley tomorrow?" asked Nana changing the subject.

"Around ten o'clock," replied Audrey, calming down. "That will give me time to work on my dress and read before we become Pinkertons again."

"Be sure to come see me after you've talked with the reverend," said their father. "I'd like to know what he thinks about Dr. Jeremiah Chetham."

CHAPTER 8

Monday 12 April 1881: "More pancakes, Brad?"

"No thanks, Nana, I'm filled up."

"Brad," Audrey interjected. "I'll wash and dry the dishes. That will give you more time to chop the wood. Then we can meet with Reverend Wesley at ten o'clock."

"Good," he replied. "I'll saddle the horses as soon as I finish chopping wood. I should have everything ready so we can leave in about half an hour."

Audrey was holding her brother's hat when he entered the house. "I saw you leading the horses out of the corral, so I got ready," said Audrey. "But, if you'd like a cup of hot tea and some oatmeal cookies first, we can wait."

"No, thanks," said Brad. "I'm too anxious about meeting with Reverend Wesley. Let's go."

"The usual race?" queried his sister.

"Of course, and I already have the prize for the winner."

"And what is that?"

"The winner receives an apple for their horse,"

"Did I hear you say the winner receives an apple for their horse?"

"Yes, and the loser receives an apple for their horse

too. The horses are doing the work, so they deserve to win something."

"Brad Benton," she exclaimed, reining in Blaze alongside Ebony. "You come up with some of the craziest things."

"One! Two! Three!" he shouted.

The horses broke into an immediate gallop toward the road. Ebony won by a head and quickly slowed to a fast trot.

"You have the apples with you?" asked Audrey.

"They're in my coat. When we reach the Wesley's, we'll give them the apples before we go in."

It wasn't long before they dismounted and looped their reins over the Wesley's hitching rail. Brad reached into his jacket pocket, retrieved two apples, and gave one to Audrey. Ebony smelled the scent of the apples and nickered.

"One for each of you," said Audrey, giving an apple to Blaze.

"No, I didn't forget you, Ebony," added Brad, giving the other one to his horse.

Brad knocked on the door and stepped back. Almost immediately, Reverend Wesley opened it.

"Come in," said the reverend. "Trevor is here, and I have the wire. Gino delivered it personally a few minutes ago."

"Come into the office," said Father O'Brien. "Nurse Davis is with Mrs. Wesley in the kitchen preparing for the birth of a new Wesley."

"Your wife is in labor?" asked Audrey, her eyes wide in amazement.

"Not yet," laughed the reverend. "She is due in a week or two, or whenever the baby is ready to come."

"They're just setting things out so when her labor begins, everything is ready," explained Father O'Brien.

"My friend in Denver says that he hasn't heard of Dr. Jeremiah Chetham," said the reverend changing the subject. "However, he said the occurrence of burglaries a few weeks before the arrival of the healer sounds like an evangelist who was in Chicago last year."

"Then Dr. Jeremiah Chetham might be a fake?" suggested Audrey.

"Not necessarily," said Father O'Brien. "But it does appear that he might the same healer that was in Chicago last year."

"How do the burglaries tie in with Dr. Jeremiah Chetham's arrival?" asked Brad.

"He has some people who appear afflicted, members of his gang we call 'plants,' move into town several weeks before his arrival," explained the reverend. "Then during his healing meeting, he miraculously cures their supposed afflictions. His plants, of course, act very grateful and immediately give him large donations. He thanks his plants, and says the donations will enable him to travel to other towns and cure other folks' afflictions."

"He doesn't cure or heal; he just pretends to heal so he can make people feel good about giving him donations. Is that right?" asked Brad.

"You understand the process," said Reverend Wesley. "The burglaries before the meeting are done by the advance men, his plants."

"What about people with real afflictions?" asked Audrey. "Doesn't he help them?"

"He tries, but fails," explained Father O'Brien. "The healer tells the people before the meeting that he won't be able to cure everyone, only some of the people. And then to add to the religious authenticity, he explains that only Jesus could cure everyone, and that he is not Jesus. He claims that he is only a faithful servant trying to help the Lord's people."

"Now I understand how a fake evangelist can be so successful," said Audrey, gently nodding her head. "He sounds so smooth, so faithful, so dedicated, so. . . so honest."

"He sounds so dedicated that some people give him their life savings," explained Father O'Brien. "Men give him their money and watches and women give him their jewelry."

"To make it worse, many times homes are burglarized while people are at the healer's meeting," said Reverend Wesley. "A healer, or evangelist, usually attracts most of the town to his meeting. With no one in the homes, his men just kick in the doors and take money, jewelry, guns, and other small valuables. Stores are also robbed, and the gang is gone before the meeting is over. The next day if folks suspect the healer, they search his wagon, but he only has what the people gave him. So, of course, they feel bad for doubting him, and sometimes give him more money as an apology."

"Riverton is being robbed by Dr. Jeremiah Chetham's gang of burglars," Brad declared. "We've got to trap them!"

"And capture them," added Audrey, rubbing her nose thoughtfully.

"I've got an idea," said Brad. "We'll be back tomorrow

with our plan. If Dr. Jeremiah Chetham is a fake, we may be able to catch him."

"Running Bear," greeted Victoria, opening the front door. "You're just in time for lunch. Will you join us?"

"Hello, Mrs. Hanson, I would like that very much," replied Running Bear, lifting a large cloth sack. "I have a large venison roast for you. Shall I put it in your cellar or in your kitchen?"

"Thank you! The kitchen will be fine," replied Victoria. I'll prepare it for supper."

He followed her to the kitchen, emptied the sack, and placed the roast in a large cast iron pan.

"Where are your Pinkertons?" he asked, a barely visible smile on his face.

"They should be home any time now. They went to Riverton to talk with Reverend Wesley about the burglaries."

"Burglaries, plural?" said Running Bear. "How many have there been?"

"There've been over ten that I know about in the past few weeks. Wash up and I'll let them tell you about it. Brad, Audrey, and Mr. Lacy were even tied up and robbed at the Big Foot Ranch last Saturday."

"I will wash quickly," said Running Bear. "I hear their horses now."

Brad was the first to see the strange horse in the corral. "Audrey, Running Bear is here."

"I know," said Audrey. "That's his horse."

"We can put our horses in the corral for now," said Brad. "Let's see why he's here."

"Brad, Audrey," greeted Running Bear, as they entered the house. "Your grandmother told me about your experience with a masked man on Saturday. You must tell me more about the burglaries."

"You can tell Running Bear about it during lunch," Nana insisted. "Wash up and have a seat. I'm putting the venison stew and biscuits on the table now."

Brad said grace and they began eating. Bear listened carefully as they told him about the robbery at the Big Foot Ranch, their house, and the other homes in Riverton.

"We talked to Reverend Wesley this morning about Dr. Jeremiah Chetham, a healer who's coming to town," said Audrey. "It is possible that his advance men are the burglars. Some afflicted people come to town several weeks before the arrival of the healer. During the evangelist's meeting, these people are miraculously healed. They are very grateful, of course, and give large donations to the healer so he can continue curing other people's afflictions."

"I am sure that you have been developing a plan," laughed Running Bear. "Do you wish to tell me about it?"

For the next hour, Brad, Audrey, Running Bear, and Nana helped develop a plan to uncover whether or not Dr. Chetham was a fake. And if his advance men were the burglars, they'd uncover that, too.

"I will ask some men to come early Saturday morning, well before sunrise," said Running Bear.

"Audrey and I will care for your warrior's horses," said Brad. "We'll take them to the Bar-X. I'm sure Hank Lacy will help us when I tell him what we need to do."

"My men will give a call like an owl," explained

Running Bear. "When the person in the house hears the owl, it will be one of my men and they can open the door."

"What about the general store?" asked Audrey. "Owls don't live in Riverton."

"It will be best if Mr. Bevins is at the store to let them in," said Running Bear. "A warrior must not be seen standing outside the general store before the first sun."

"It's a good plan," confirmed Nana. "Your men and my grandchildren will certainly capture some burglars next Saturday night. Now don't forget to take those two deer hides we have tacked to the side of the barn."

"I will not forget," said Running Bear. Looking directly at Audrey, he continued. "You have done much for my people. The women of my village have told me they wish to make a set of buckskins for you. Next month, I will bring you the buckskins. You will become an honorary Indian, an honorary blond Indian."

"Running Bear!" exclaimed Audrey. "A set of buckskins! I can hardly wait. I am honored that they will make me a set. Please thank them. And next month, I will come to your village and thank them personally."

"I'll help you get the hides," said Brad, going to the back door. "I have to unsaddle the horses and clean the barn."

"I'll take off their bridles," said Audrey. "And give them their oats."

Brad and Audrey said their final good-byes to Running Bear. Bear nodded to Nana, standing on the front porch, and urged his horse into a lope, heading home to his village.

CHAPTER 9

Tuesday, 13 April 1881: Brad and his sister looped their reins over the Wesley's hitching rail. Together, they went up to the front door and paused. Slowly, Brad lifted his right hand, and knocked.

"Do you think he'll like the plan?" Audrey whispered, nervously.

"We'll know in a minute, I hear him coming now."

"We've been expecting you," the reverend said. "Trevor and I have been talking about our Easter services."

"How is your wife?" asked Audrey.

"She's due to deliver in the next few weeks," said the reverend. "Doc Adams said she can begin labor any day now, but next week is most likely. Trevor and I are doing most of the household duties so she can stay off her feet."

"I'm tired," said Mrs. Wesley, coming to greet Brad and Audrey. "But not so tired that I couldn't bake a chocolate cake. Let's meet in the kitchen."

When they were seated, Reverend Wesley said, "Tell us about your plan. And while you're doing that, I'll cut us some cake."

"I'll pour the coffee and tea," said Audrey, quickly standing up and going to the stove.

"Thank you, Audrey," said Mrs. Wesley. "I do appreciate your help."

"Well," said Brad, picking up his fork. "We believe that Dr. Jeremiah Chetham is a fake and his advance men are the burglars. We also believe that there will be a number of burglaries the night of his healing meeting."

"You said, 'we,'" observed Father O'Brien. "You usually just say 'Audrey and I'. Am I to conclude that your plan was created with additional help?"

Brad swallowed a bite of cake, and said, "Yes, Nana and Running Bear helped us. I think that we created a very good plan."

"Please continue," said the reverend.

"Running Bear and some of his braves will come to Riverton early Saturday morning. They'll go into the homes and businesses before dawn, so no one will see them. They'll stay hidden all day. When the people leave their homes and shops to go to the healer's meeting, the braves will remain hidden inside."

"Then if, or when, the burglars break into the house, the braves will be able to capture them," said Audrey.

"What about the captured burglars?" asked the reverend.

"We thought we could jail them at the train depot's warehouse," Brad explained, "just like Uncle Henry did with the Badger Gang."

"If the healer really is a healer, the effort will have been in vain," Audrey concluded. This way no one will be falsely accused."

"I like this plan," said Reverend Wesley. "What about you, Trevor?"

"It is a good plan. I like it, too."

"Your plan provides for Dr. Chetham being a real healer," said Reverend Wesley. "Do you believe he can perform miracles and is a real healer?"

"No," said Brad. "I believe he is a fake."

"I think so, too," added Audrey. But, if he is a real healer and can miraculously cure afflictions, we don't want to be like the priests at the temple who falsely accused Jesus."

"There is much merit in your position," said Father O'Brien. "Bob and I do not want to be like the priests that demanded the crucifixion of Jesus."

"Do you think Dr. Jeremiah Chetham is a fake?" asked Brad.

"Yes," said Father O'Brien. "I do."

"And so do I," added the reverend. "I also agree that his advance men are the burglars."

During the next half-hour, they made a list of Riverton's residents and stores that would be likely targets of the burglars. Brad, of course, had a second piece of cake, and Audrey and Father O'Brien quickly washed the dishes.

There was a knock at the door. "I wonder who that could be," said Reverend Wesley as he went to the door. "Doc Adams! I wasn't expecting you until this afternoon. Do come in."

"I have to go out to Bar-X," said the doctor. "One of Hank Lacy's men got knocked around by a steer. Since I may be at the ranch the rest of the day, I thought I'd better stop by and check on Martha now."

"Come into the bedroom," said Mrs. Wesley. "Is it all right if Audrey comes along?"

"Why, sure, she should learn how to deliver a baby.

If you have no objection, perhaps she could help with the delivery."

"Object?" said Mrs. Wesley. "I wouldn't object. I'd like her to be here. Would you help in the delivery, Audrey?"

"Of course, I've never seen a baby born before."

"Then it's settled," said the doctor. "We'll get word to you as soon as Martha begins labor, and you can help us deliver the baby."

After leaving the Wesley's, Brad and Audrey walked their horses down Main Street. They stopped in front of the general store and looped their reins over the hitching rail.

"Let's talk to Mr. Bevins," said Brad, as they entered the store. "I'm sure he'll be agreeable to our plan."

"Brad, Audrey," greeted Wilma Sue. "Give me your list, and I'll fill your order."

"We came to talk to your Pa today, no list," said Audrey. "Is he here?"

"He's in the storeroom arranging the stock," said Wilma Sue. "We received a shipment first thing this morning and he's straightening things up."

When they reached the dock, Brad picked up a small keg of nails and said, "Mr. Bevins, we have a plan we'd like to discuss with you."

"Alright, but I need to keep putting things away."

"Sure," said Brad, setting down the keg of nails. "I'll help, and Audrey will explain the plan."

By the time everything was put away, Audrey had finished describing the plan. Mr. Bevins and Brad sat down on some bags of horse feed and looked at Audrey.

"It sounds good," remarked Mr. Bevins. "I'll explain

it to Edith and Wilma Sue tonight. We won't say a word about it to anyone."

"Thank you," Audrey smiled. "We'll be able to give you more details later in the week."

As they removed the reins from the hitching rail, Audrey said, "Let's see Mr. Acker next. Then it will be time to go home for lunch."

Brad stopped in front of the door marked PRIVATE. He gave a short knock and said, "Mr. Acker, its Brad and Audrey Benton."

"Come in."

As they entered his office, he motioned them to a couple of chairs in front of his desk. "What can I do for Riverton's two Pinkertons? Am I correct that it's about the burglaries?"

"You're correct, as usual," replied Audrey.

"Am I also correct in that you have a plan to catch the burglars?"

"Again, you are correct," said Brad, smiling.

"Now for the final guess," said Mr. Acker, leaning forward. "Do you believe the burglaries are related to the coming of Dr. Jeremiah Chetham?"

"I don't know how you do it," said Audrey, shaking her head. "You must read minds."

"Not really," said Mr. Acker. "But I do possess the power of observation, the same as you. Since I am older, and more experienced, I usually arrive at the same conclusion you do, but possibly with less effort."

Brad and Audrey looked at each other, confused, and then back at Mr. Acker. Before they could speak, he continued, "Don't misinterpret what I said. You have the ability to see things clearly and put the pieces of a puzzle together. It is an ability that very few of Riverton's citizens possess. Reverend Wesley and Father O'Brien also have that ability. I don't know anyone else in Riverton who has it. Now, I'm sure you have a plan. What can I do to help you?"

Brad and Audrey explained their plan. Mr. Acker was quiet for a while, turned his swivel chair to the left, and then to the right. Finally, he faced them and said, "I like it. I'll also provide coffee and sandwiches to your jailers."

"Jailers?" Brad asked.

"Someone is going to have to guard the burglars you catch," said Mr. Acker. "And, you'll catch quite a few; I expect it will be more than ten. You have a big operation planned and I'm sure we're going to be successful. I, too, have had items of value stolen from my hotel. I just haven't told Sheriff Tate."

"You've had things stolen, too?" Audrey said in disbelief.

"I suggest we call them the 'Passover Bandits'," said Mr. Acker, a twinkle in his eye.

"What do you mean by Passover?" asked Brad.

"Passover is a Jewish holiday that celebrates the Jews' liberation from slavery in Egypt. That is the holiday Jesus was celebrating at what you call The Last Supper. A few of the Jewish priests were corrupt and saw him as a threat; they were afraid of him. They had him brought before Pontius Pilate and demanded his execution. He was crucified on Friday, which you call Good Friday. Christians say he was resurrected on Sunday, a day which you call Easter Sunday."

"Don't you believe he was resurrected?" asked Brad.

"I believe that Jesus was a great prophet," said Mr. Acker. "Christians believe that he was resurrected, Jews do not."

"Oh," said Brad.

"But what is important," said Mr. Acker, "is that Jews and Christians both believe in the Old Testament and in the importance of adhering to the Ten Commandments. The healer and his advance men obviously don't believe in either. A society cannot survive if theft and dishonesty are a part its culture. That is what sealed the fate of the cities of Sodom and Gomorrah."

"You should be a preacher," said Audrey.

"I am," replied Mr. Acker, a twinkle in his eye. "I'm a Jewish preacher."

Brad and Audrey headed home. Once they reached the edge of town, they clucked their horses to a trot. Audrey was the first to speak. "So Mr. Acker has had things stolen from his hotel."

"I never expected him to offer food for the jailers," said Brad.

"That's just the kind of man he is," replied Audrey.

"After lunch, we'll go to the Bar-X and then to the Hodges'," said Brad. "And early tomorrow morning, we'll ride out to Running Bear's village and see how many braves will help us."

"There's the ranch house and corral," said Audrey as their horses loped down the trail to the Bar-X.

"And I see Doc Adams' buggy," added Brad. "That means Mr. Lacy is probably there, not out on the range. I forgot to ask you, how was the birthing lesson this morning?”

“There was so much! I’ll never be able to remember all of it.”

“If you’re able to assist when Mrs. Wesley gives birth, that will help you remember. It would be like a test, but the teacher would be helping you with the answers.”

“I hadn’t thought of it that way,” said Audrey as they halted at the hitching rail. “That way I don’t have to worry about failing the test. And he said I could come with him on some other deliveries, too.”

“Welcome to the Bar-X,” said Hank Lacy, coming out of the bunkhouse. “I heard you ride up, came out to see who it was.”

“We’d like to have a talk with you,” Brad said, “in private.”

“Sure, let’s go over by the corral. We can talk there without being overheard.”

When they reached the corral, Brad said, “We’d like your help in catching the burglars.”

“Do you know who they are?” asked Hank.

“We don’t know for sure,” said Brad. “But we’re pretty confident. That’s why we need your help.”

“Of course, I’ll help you,” said Hank. “What do you need me to do?”

Brad and Audrey explained the plan. Hank listened carefully and then said, “I’ll bring the horses to our corral. I’ll tell the men that I’m thinking of buying them and that Running Bear will be out Sunday afternoon to meet with me.”

“We’re going to Running Bear’s village tomorrow,” said Brad.

"Then be sure to tell him that the horses we take on Saturday morning need to be good horses," said Hank. "No need to make any of my men suspicious."

"Doc Adams just came out of the bunk house." Audrey nodded toward the doctor.

They walked over to him as he was putting his bag in the buggy. "Your man will be fine in a few days," said the doctor. "But he's to do no riding or hard work until next week. He can repair tack and other light tasks."

"There is always plenty of tack to care for," said Hank. "I'm sorry I asked you to come all the way out here for what wasn't a desperate situation."

"You didn't know," said the doctor. "And I didn't know either, until after I had examined him. Don't forget that he didn't regain consciousness until after I arrived."

"If you're going back to Riverton," said Brad, "we'll ride with you."

"I'd like that," he said, a brief smile crossed the doctor's face as he climbed into the buggy. "One never knows when Big Foot might appear, and there's safety in numbers."

"We could use Big Foot's help in capturing the burglars," joked Hank. "If you see him on the way back, ask him if he'll help us."

"We'll do that," laughed Brad, reining in Ebony beside the buggy."

Once away from the ranch, Doc Adams slapped the reins, and his horse broke into a quick trot, a pace that didn't change until they reached the edge of Riverton.

CHAPTER 10

Wednesday, 14 April 1881: "Have a nice ride out to Running Bear's village," said Nana, as Brad and Audrey clucked their horses to a trot. In a short period time they had reached the road and turned north.

"It sure is pretty this morning," observed Brad. "The sun feels nice, too."

"The worst of the winter is over," said Audrey.

"We'll probably still get a few more storms, maybe even a big one."

"I doubt we'll get another one big enough to close school for a week."

"It's a long trip to Bear's village, we'd best hurry. Running Bear said he would be at their school this morning doing some cleaning and repairing." They gently urged their horses to a lope, doubling their speed. As they neared the school building, they slowed them to a walk.

"There's smoke coming from the chimney," said Audrey. "He must be there."

They stopped, tethering their horses to some small saplings. Audrey removed a cloth bag from her saddlebag, and they went to the schoolhouse. Brad turned the doorknob and they went inside. It was a small, one-room schoolhouse with a pot-bellied stove in the center. Running Bear was building some shelves in a closet and Gentle Water was mopping the floor.

"Good morning, Running Bear, Gentle Water," said Brad, standing just inside the doorway. "Are we too early?"

"No," replied Running Bear. "You arrive at a most opportune moment. It is time for us to take a break."

"Come," said Gentle Water, motioning to some chairs next to the teacher's desk. "I have made tea for us."

"Thank you, Gentle Water," said Audrey, pulling up a chair.

"Yes," said Brad. "Thank you."

Gentle Water poured tea into four mugs, and then returned the blue enamel coffeepot to the back of the stove. Audrey opened the cloth bag and removed a tin plate and a number of oatmeal cookies. Running Bear bowed his head and thanked the Lord for Brad and Audrey's safe journey and for the food before them.

"Nana's oatmeal cookies!" exclaimed Brad. "Audrey, why didn't you tell me?"

"Victoria wanted the cookies to reach the school," teased Running Bear.

"That's right," said Audrey. "Nana said not to tell you or you'd eat them before we got out of the corral."

"Well," said Brad sheepishly, "I probably would have waited until we were on the road."

"You are a growing boy," said Running Bear. "You will become bigger than your father, and your father is a big man."

"He will make an excellent husband for some lucky woman," announced Audrey. "When we searched for

Pa, he built the fire and had a cup of hot tea ready for me when I woke up."

"I have many sisters who would like to be your squaw," said Gentle Water, with a giggle.

"I, uh, I'm not ready to get married," insisted Brad, his face reddening.

"We tease you, my friend," said Running Bear. "But your sister is correct. You will make some woman a fine husband. Take your time. Do not rush into marriage. Many snows will pass before you are ready for marriage. And maybe we can capture some burglars first."

"Yes," said Brad. "Let's capture some burglars."

"I have twelve braves, one squaw, and myself, who will help you the day before Easter," said Running Bear.

"That's a lot of help," said Audrey. "Thank you."

"Yes," said Brad, pulling a sheet of paper out of his pocket. "We have a list of homes and businesses where we think the burglars will strike Saturday night."

As they studied the list, Running Bear asked questions, recommending a specific warrior for each home. Gentle Water nodded in agreement with most of his decisions but suggested that Trader should be at the Bevinses' home and Short Bull at the general store.

"Now we need several braves to help guard the prisoners," said Brad. "We'll hold them at the train depot warehouse, the same place the Badger Gang was kept."

"I know it well," recalled Running Bear. "That would be an excellent assignment for Forest Water; she is very good with wounds. Strong Warrior and White Elk are both very strong and should be at the depot. You said

86

Buckley Hodges volunteered to guard the prisoners. He will need some very strong men."

"We don't want anyone to get hurt," said Audrey.

"When capturing bad men, expect some men to be hurt," advised Running Bear. "Now, please tell the homeowners to expect to hear three hoots of an owl sometime before dawn."

"That will be before five in the morning," said Brad, scrunching his face in thought.

"The braves at the general store will rub the door with a small tree branch. Mr. Bevins should listen for the sound of the tree branch."

"A tree branch," Audrey repeated thoughtfully.

"Each brave will have food and water with him, so they can remain hidden all day, whether in a home or in a business," said Running Bear.

"Thank you for the written list," said Running Bear. "I will show it to my students next week so they will see a practical application of reading and writing."

"Yes," added Gentle Water. "The hunting days of the Indian are numbered. We must teach our children how to read and write."

"Please tell your friends that the night of Good Friday they may hear or see some braves around their farms and ranches," said Running Bear. "They must not be afraid. My braves will give the hoot of an owl if they are challenged, but will not come to the house until the hour before dawn."

As they prepared to leave, Brad said, "Gentle Water. "Thank you for the tea."

"Yes, thank you," said Audrey.

"Running Bear," said Brad, grasping his friend's

hand, "Thank you for your help. We may expose a fake healer and capture some burglars."

"Until Saturday," replied Running Bear, as Brad and Audrey mounted their horses.

"Please thank Victoria for the oatmeal cookies," said Gentle Water.

"We will," replied Audrey, as they nudged their horses to a lope.

Wednesday Afternoon: "That was a long ride out to Bear's village," observed Reverend Wesley. "Father O'Brien is making a call on a new family that arrived last week. They're a young couple from Ireland. We believe they're Catholic, so he's the best one to visit them."

"I'll pour the tea today," said Mrs. Wesley, filling the mugs. "I'll let you pour it after the baby comes, that's when I can really use the help. But for now, tell us about your visit with Running Bear."

"Running Bear is sending twelve braves, one squaw who is a nurse, and himself," said Brad, finishing his piece of cake. Mrs. Wesley quickly put another slice on Brad's plate.

"That is quite a number of special deputies," commented Reverend Wesley. "Tell me more."

Brad and Audrey explained about the three hoots of an owl and the signal of a tree branch rubbing on the door. Audrey made a copy of the list showing where each brave was assigned as they discussed the plan. Reverend Wesley made a few additional suggestions to which Brad and Audrey quickly agreed.

"I think we have a good plan," the reverend concluded.

"If you ride fast, you should be able to bring Hank Lacy up to date on the plan and be back in time for supper."

"I'll certainly be ready for supper," said Brad, following his sister to the front door. "This is a long day, and its only early afternoon."

Brad and Audrey walked their horses to the south side of town and then let the horses settle into a comfortable lope to the Bar-X. They tied their horses to the corral rail at the water trough while they talked to Hank Lacy.

"It's agreed, then," said Hank. "We'll meet at the grove of trees, just south of town, early Saturday morning. I'll have a small fire going. The three of us will bring the horses out here for a couple of days."

"Thanks, Mr. Lacy," said Brad. "We'll see you then."

Brad and Audrey mounted their horses for their return to Riverton. At the edge of town, they slowed their horses to a walk, then returned to a lope on the other side until they reached the lane to their home.

"Brad," said Audrey. "We've got to walk the horses, let them cool down."

"We're going to have to wipe them down, too," said Brad.

Brad opened the corral gate, and the horses went directly into the barn. He removed their saddles while Audrey put an extra-large scoop of oats in their feed troughs. Using some old towels, they wiped down the horses.

"I'm tired," declared Brad. "This has been a long day with lots of riding. We didn't even have lunch, just a snack at Bear's village and a slice of cake this afternoon with Reverend Wesley."

"It must be late," said Audrey. "I think I see Pa coming down the lane."

Brad looked at the position of the sun, then at their father walking down the lane. "It sure is, we'd better go help Nana with dinner."

"I'm sorry we're late, Nana," said Audrey as they burst through the kitchen door. "After we left Running Bear's village..."

"Your Ma and I expected you to be late. You were working hard. We've got the table set, and dinner is ready. Your Pa should be home any minute. Now go wash up."

"Pa is coming down the lane now," said Brad, pushing the pump handle for his sister.

"Thanks for understanding," said Audrey. "We..."

"Wait until dinner," said their mother. "We want your Pa to hear too. He's already on the front porch."

A few minutes later, Harold Benton said "Amen" and everyone raised their head. "Venison stew and cornbread; you must have a new stew pot, Victoria."

"Abby and I got it when we walked to town this morning," said Victoria. "We knew the venison ribs wouldn't last another day. Harold, I don't think we're going to see my stew pot again. It's gone, forever. And we're not so poor that we can't afford a new one."

"I'd forgotten all about the stew pot," said Harold. "I'm glad you got a new one. I talked with Sheriff Tate this afternoon; there were more burglaries last night."

"Any new evidence, Pa?" asked Audrey.

"Nothing - the sheriff is discouraged. He asked me if my Pinkertons had any new leads and I said nothing as of last night."

"Well," drawled Brad. "We don't have any new leads, but we do have a trap that we'll set on Saturday. Reverend Wesley, Father O'Brien, Mr. Acker, and Hank Lacy have checked the plan and are helping," said Brad.

"And Running Bear has twelve braves and a nurse who will help, too," added Audrey.

Their father stopped, his fork half-way to his mouth, and looked at Brad. Slowly, he turned is head and looked at his daughter. The room was silent as their mother and Nana, their mouths open, looked at Brad and Audrey, and then at Harold Benton.

"It must be a magnificent plan if all those folks have bought into it," said their father, a big grin spreading across his face. "I expect I have a part in your plan. Tell me about it."

Brad and Audrey explained the plan in detail to their father. When they finished, their father said, "It is a very ambitious plan. However, it is based on the presumption that the burglaries and Dr. Chetham are connected."

"We know, Pa," replied Brad. "Everyone knows that, and they agreed to help. They want to catch the burglars."

"I hope you catch those burglars," declared Nana. "But I have an important question, how is Mrs. Wesley?"

"She is due any day," answered Audrey. "And, Doc Adams and Mrs. Wesley asked me to help at the delivery. As I said the other day, I even helped him examine Mrs. Wesley, and he explained what I should do."

"Isn't Nurse Davis going to help?" asked her mother.

"Yes, but he said I should know how to deliver a

baby. He could be out of town, and Nurse Davis may need some help."

"You can never learn too much," affirmed their grandmother. "You'll make a fine nurse, if that's what you want. You'd also make a good doctor, if you can find a medical school that admits women."

"I never thought about being a nurse, or a doctor," said Audrey. "College would cost a lot of money."

"If you keep catching outlaws, you'll have more than enough reward money to pay your college expenses," laughed their grandmother.

"Back to the burglaries. We've got to visit Sheriff Tate tomorrow," said Brad. "He needs to be brought up to date with the plan."

"He's got to know how we're going to expose Dr. Jeremiah Chetham as a fake," said Audrey.

"Are you sure that Dr. Chetham is a fake?" asked their father.

"We really believe he is a fake," said Brad. "But we have to prove it."

"You're not going to call him a fake, without proof, are you?"

"No," replied Audrey. "We might be wrong and he might be a real healer. That's why we have so many people helping. However, everyone we talk to believes he is a fake."

"So do I, but you can't accuse a man of being dishonest without proof, conclusive proof."

"We will have conclusive proof before his meeting is over," replied Audrey.

"You'd better get some rest then," he advised. "You left before I did this morning, spent all day riding, and missed lunch. You have to be exhausted. Do your chores and head to bed."

"We will, Pa," said Brad, picking up the dishes.

"I'm going to bed as soon as we're through with the dishes," said Audrey, yawning.

CHAPTER 11

Saturday 17 April 1881: Victoria was up, listening intently. The sun hadn't risen yet, but from the kitchen window she was just able to see the outline of the trees and the barn. The Indians should arrive very shortly. She added another stick of wood to the cook stove and filled the teakettle and coffeepot. Then she heard it - an owl hooting three times.

She opened the door a crack and heard a voice say, "Victoria, Running Bear sent us. I am Lone Wolf," said the brave, "and this is White Crow."

"Come in," she said softly, opening the door all the way.

"I'll get Brad and Audrey, then we'll have breakfast.

Brad heard voices, sat up in bed, and heard Nana's familiar footsteps in the hall.

She knocked softly on the door, "Brad, it's time to get up. Lone Wolf and White Crow are here; breakfast will be ready in a bit."

Brad dressed quickly. In the dim pre-dawn light, he rinsed his face with water from his pitcher and basin and headed downstairs.

"Morning, Nana, Lone Wolf, White Crow," said Brad. "Thank you for coming."

"Running Bear said very important we come,"

replied Lone Wolf. "Help you catch men who take things from you."

"That is the plan," said Brad. "No one must know that you are here. Your horses can be tied in the barn, or I can take them with me to the Bar-X. We must not let them be seen in the corral or field."

"Horses once belong to Big Foot Ranch," said White Crow. "They like barn with hay and water."

"Since they'll be in our barn, I'll add some oats and apples," said Audrey, entering the kitchen.

Brad and Audrey explained that in the evening they would leave for the healer's meeting. The house must look like no one is home. If they guessed correctly, the burglars would come shortly after they left. Lone Wolf and White Crow said they would capture any men that might come.

"Now the man, or men, will be armed," warned Brad. "They tied up Hank Lacy, Audrey, and me last Saturday at the Big Foot Ranch."

"They will hear and see nothing," declared Lone Wolf.

"They will wake up in your jail," stated White Crow.

"That is where they belong," said Nana, stacking pancakes on a platter. "Buckley Hodges will be at the warehouse with two braves waiting for you. How will you get them there?"

"Tie men up, wrap in blankets, use travois," said Lone Wolf. "There are many ways to take men to warehouse."

"You can ride down Main Street with them if they're gagged, tied, and wrapped in blankets," said Brad. "No one would suspect a thing."

"That what Running Bear say," said White Crow, flashing a fiendish smile.

"Breakfast is ready," said Nana. "I expect you're quite hungry after your ride from your village.

"Yes," said Lone Wolf."

Brad said grace, and everyone began to eat. Victoria poured coffee, and Audrey poured the tea. Brad and Audrey ate quickly and headed to the barn. Audrey held the lantern while Brad saddled Blaze and Ebony and gave oats and apples to the Indian's horses.

"Dawn will arrive in less than an hour," said Brad, as they mounted their horses. "We've got to hurry."

The horses started for Riverton at a lope. They slowed to a trot when they reached the edge of town and then to a slow walk as they went to the rear of Bevins's General Store.

"Morning, Brad, Audrey," said Mr. Bevins. "Short Bull has arrived. You can take his horse."

"See you tonight," said Audrey, as Brad took the horse's lead.

The stop took less than a minute. Brad clucked to Ebony. They returned to Main Street and headed at a slow trot to the train depot warehouse. Zeke, a Bar-X ranch hand, was waiting for them, holding the leads of four horses tied to a long rope.

"Morning, Miss Benton, Brad," said Zeke. "These are the four horses Mr. Lacy said you'd be picking up."

"Thanks, Zeke," said Brad, "and thanks for tying them to a rope."

"I told him it's a lot easier that way," said Zeke, "and he agreed. Pleased you like it."

Brad gently nudged Ebony to a lope as they headed out of town. Audrey followed him for a bit, in case one of the horses tried to break away.

"Mr. Lacy should have dropped Dooley off at Reverend Wesley's by now," said Audrey, coming alongside her brother. "I'm cold, I can't wait to get to Mr. Lacy's fire."

"We'll find out in a minute," said Brad, patting Ebony on her neck. "The grove of trees is just around that bend."

Moments later Audrey said, "I see the light of the fire. It's about a half-mile ahead."

As they approached the grove, they reined their horses to a slow trot, and then a walk.

"Mr. Lacy isn't back yet," said Brad, dismounting. "I'll tether the horses."

"I'll add a couple of sticks to the fire," said Audrey, a quiver in her voice from the cold.

By the time Brad had tethered the horses, the newly added wood was burning, and Audrey was seated on an old tree stump next to the fire.

After a while, Audrey stood up. "I hear horses."

"That should be Mr. Lacy," said Brad.

A moment later a lone rider leading two horses came around the bend in the road. As the rider neared the grove of trees with the fire, he slowed and headed toward them.

"Morning, Brad, Audrey. It looks like we have seven horses to take to the Bar-X."

"Want to warm up first, or head out?" asked Audrey.

"I think I'd like to warm up first," he said, as Brad tethered the horses. "I've been riding for over an hour."

"I added some wood to the fire," said Audrey. "I was pretty sure you'd be ready to warm up after that early-morning ride."

"That feels mighty nice," he said, crouching by the

fire. "I didn't see anyone this morning, other than the reverend. How about you?"

"Mr. Bevins and Zeke are the only folks we saw," said Brad. "Everyone else is just now getting out of bed."

"We ought to get going," said Mr. Lacy. "I'd rather not have anyone see us leading seven horses, five of which are Indian horses, this time of the morning."

"They'd probably ask questions and talk," said Brad, kicking some dirt on the remains of the fire. Hank emptied the water from his canteen on the mound of dirt, creating a surge of steam.

"Does Cookie make tea in the morning?" asked Audrey wistfully.

"Rarely," said Hank, mounting his horse. "But this morning is one of those rarities: I told him you and Brad were coming out for a second breakfast."

Two Indians reined their horses to a halt in front of the sheriff's office, dismounted, and entered. "I guess it's that time," said Sheriff Tate standing. "Come on back and make yourselves comfortable. What are your names?"

"Bull Bear," said the larger Indian. He was about six feet tall and weighed over 200 pounds. He had neatly cropped black hair and wore tan buckskins and a gun belt.

"Thunder," said the smaller Indian, his full, resonant voice matching his name. He, too, wore buckskins and a gun belt.

"I'll have to take your gun belts," said the sheriff. "It

wouldn't look right for you to be in jail wearing your six-shooters. If you have a knife, keep it hidden."

"Running Bear said you would take our guns," said Thunder, unbuckling his gun belt.

"I'll put them in my bottom desk drawer," said the sheriff. "And I have a key for your cell. Let me show you how to use it."

Bull Bear and Thunder watched Sheriff Tate unlock the cell door.

"Now go into the cell and practice unlocking it through the bars," said the sheriff, closing the door, and locking it.

Thunder took the key and slowly inserted it, unlocking the cell door.

"You're next, Bull Bear," said the sheriff.

Bull Bear took the key, reached his hand through the bars, inserted the key, turned it, and opened the cell door.

"Good," said the sheriff, relocking the cell door. "Get yourselves comfortable and keep that key hidden. I'm going over to the Riverton Hotel and will bring you back some breakfast, courtesy of Mr. Acker."

"Will that include his special blend coffee?" asked Bull Bear, putting the key in the pocket of his buckskins.

"I'll bring back an entire pot for you," said the sheriff, smiling. "While I'm gone, sprinkle a little of this whiskey on yourselves. You were drunk and disorderly last night, that's why you're in jail."

"We don't drink firewater," protested Bull Bear.

"Good, don't start. It's one of Satan's temptations."

"That's the call of the hoot owl," said Buck. "I'll open the back door."

Two Indians stood several yards away from the door. "Buck Hodges, Jr.?" one of them asked.

"Yes," replied Buck. "Running Bear said you would be here around dawn. Please come in."

The two Indians entered the back door of the Hodges' ranch house, stopped, and looked around the kitchen. "I am Singing Coyote," said a rather thin Indian.

"I am Walker," said the other Indian. "Our horses are in your barn where they will not be seen."

"Thank you," said Buck. "Pa asked me to have you put them there. He said some folks may stop by to pick up their guns today: A rifle, shotgun, and two pistols."

"I don't know what you usually have for breakfast," said Mrs. Hodges. "I have pancakes, eggs, ham, and coffee."

"That is good," said Coyote. "My squaw usually gives me dried meat and pemmican for morning food."

Wilma Sue sat in the kitchen, talking softly with her mother about Dr. Jeremiah Chetham. "I don't know what to believe," said Wilma Sue. "Can he really heal people with afflictions?"

"We'll see tonight," said her mother. "If he heals folks, and cures the stiffness in my hands, I'll believe he's a healer."

"And if he cures other folks, but not you, will you still believe he's a healer?"

Edith Bevins never got a chance to answer, for the hooting of an owl caused them to stop talking.

"I'll get the door, Ma," said Wilma Sue.

"I'll get breakfast ready for them."

"Spotted Owl?" said Wilma Sue, looking around the back yard.

"Miss Bevins," said Spotted Owl, standing up from behind the garden fence. "I am here."

"Come in," said Wilma Sue. "Are you alone?"

"No, I am here, too," said a second Indian, coming from behind a tree. "I am Trader."

The two Indians entered the Bevinses' house and were quickly greeted by Mrs. Bevins. "Good morning, just call me Edith. You've already met my daughter, Wilma Sue."

"I'm sure you're hungry after the long night," said Mrs. Bevins. "I'll have breakfast ready for you in a few minutes. Please have a seat." Edith motioned them to two empty chairs at the kitchen table.

"Our horses are in trees," said Spotted Owl. "Running Bear say horses must not be seen."

"After breakfast, why don't you move them into the barn?" suggested Edith. "There's hay, water, and oats for them."

"I'll bring up some carrots for them, too," said Wilma Sue. "Brad Benton says his horse likes them."

"Horse of Brad Benton is black one," Spotted Owl explained to Trader. "His horse like carrots, then our horses like carrots."

Mrs. Bevins set a platter of pancakes on the table and then picked up a plate of fried eggs and bacon. Wilma Sue took the pot of coffee from the stove and filled everyone's mugs.

Spotted Owl looked around the room and said, "I say

grace." He bowed his head, as did Trader. Wilma Sue and her mother bowed their heads, and Spotted Owl said, "Lord, thank you for fine food. Please help us do as Running Bear ask. Amen."

The sun was up and a pheasant, startled by the horses, ran across the road. "There's the trail to the Bar-X," said Brad.

"I'm ready for some of Cookie's tea," said Audrey.

"All of us are," added Hank. "It's been a cold morning. I'm hungry, too."

"You haven't had breakfast yet?" questioned Brad.

"No. Cookie said he'd be waiting for us. Said he'd expect us about an hour after sunrise. The men will have had breakfast by then and he'll have his kitchen table set and waiting for us with pancakes, bacon, eggs, and a large pot of hot tea."

"I'm ready for a second breakfast!" declared Brad.

Audrey hesitated. "Well, since I had a small breakfast, I can certainly have a little, especially some tea."

CHAPTER 12

Saturday Evening: It was early evening as Jake Jackson walked around the school meeting room, lighting the kerosene lamps. This was his job for evening and weekend meetings at the school.

Gino Donatelli had eaten supper, said good-bye to his wife, and had walked to the school. He lived in town, close to the train depot, so he didn't need to own a horse.

"Evening," said the sheriff, as Gino entered the meeting room. "You're here early."

"Yes, Sheriff, I wanted to get a front row seat. I want to hear everything."

"I've reserved my seat," said the sheriff, placing his hand on the back of a chair. There was a sign tied to it in bold, underlined letters:

Reserved for Sheriff Tate

"Harold, Abby, Victoria," greeted the sheriff. "Welcome to the healer's meeting. Harold, I'd like you to sit here, on the aisle. And, here's your deputy's badge. Pin it on so everyone can see it."

"Richard," asked Victoria. "Your making Harold a deputy doesn't mean you're expecting trouble, does it?"

"Nope, but it pays to be ready."

"Harold," remarked Mrs. Benton. "Now I know why you strapped on your gun belt before we left tonight."

The last customer left the general store, and Mr. Bevins bolted the front door. As he pulled down the shades, he called upstairs. "Everyone's gone, Hank. You and Short Bull can come down now."

"That's a nice storeroom you have upstairs, John," commented Hank. "That bed and overstuffed chair make it real comfortable."

"I put the bed and chair up there so that if I got caught in a storm, I'd have a place to stay. I should add a second bed since Wilma Sue and my wife, Edith, are here so much."

"Same as a line shack," said Hank. "We have a little shack with a stove, wood, and some food in the south part of our range. We're planning on making the Big Foot Ranch house a large line shack for our northern range."

"I'd better be going," said Mr. Bevins. "Sheriff Tate expects me at the meeting. Edith brought extra sandwiches and some apples this morning. The sack is behind the stove. And I've got a fresh pot of coffee and two mugs on the table. You'd best eat while there is still some light."

"Say hello to Edith and thank her for the food she made for us," said Hank.

"We're leaving for the church," said Brad. "We'll see you later tonight."

"Be careful," answered White Crow, "Bad men dangerous when cornered. Fight like badgers."

"We'll be careful," said Audrey. "Mr. Acker will be there too."

"Thank you for good food," said Lone Wolf, patting his stomach. "We ready."

Brad and Audrey went to the barn for their horses. Brad saddled them while Audrey gave some apples to the Indians' horses.

"I brought one for you too, Ebony," said Brad, giving her an apple. "You're last because it's polite to serve your guests first."

When the horses were saddled, Brad led them out of the corral and closed the gate. They mounted and headed to Riverton at a comfortable trot. When they reached the edge of town, they slowed to a walk and turned toward the church. Before they reached the church, they turned into the woods, stopped, and dismounted. They tethered the horses to some saplings before walking to the church.

"You have the key, don't you?" asked Audrey.

"Reverend Wesley's personal key," said Brad. "I see someone at the door."

"Evening, Audrey, Brad," said Mr. Acker. "I saw you ride into the woods."

As they entered the church, Brad asked, "What's valuable in the church?"

"Your faith is the most valuable item, and that resides in your heart, not a building," answered Mr. Acker. "But, don't forget the silver candlesticks, and Father O'Brien's silver sacrament service."

"I'll cover the front door," said Brad.

"I see you're wearing a gun belt," commented Audrey.

"I also brought my derringer for you," said Mr. Acker handing the small pistol to Audrey. "This is the same one that caused Duke Badger to drop his pistol in Chicago. I hope we don't need it."

Buck Hodges helped his mother into the buckboard, climbed up beside her, and slapped the reins. The horse quickly settled in to a trot.

"Ma, do you think Dr. Jeremiah Chetham can really help folks?"

"We'll find out tonight," said his mother. "My arm has been hurting for months. Doc Adams said it's from hard work and old age. He couldn't do anything for it."

"You're not old," said Buck.

"I'm not as young as I used to be. Getting old, stiff, and sore is just part of life. I'm glad the Lord has given me what I have. I have you, your father, and our friends."

"We'll be there in a little, Ma. I hope Pa's all right."

"Don't worry about your Pa. He's been in terrible situations and survived. He survived the war and a shootout with rustlers. He'll do just fine."

"I know," said Buck. "But I'll feel better when I see him."

"I will too," she confided.

"I'll drop you at the school and then go to the Riverton Hotel. I've got to pick up a couple of crates and take them to Pa at the warehouse."

"When you see your Pa, you'll understand what I mean when I said that he's fine," she promised.

106

"Thank you for hitching up the buggy for me, Spotted Owl," said Mrs. Bevins. "Wilma Sue and I appreciate it."

"If I didn't," replied Spotted Owl, "Running Bear would make me stay after school."

"Yes," said Trader. "If we not hitch horse to buggy, Running Bear have us clean erasers long time."

"Running Bear is nice," said Wilma Sue. "He wouldn't do that."

"Running Bear is our chief today," replied Spotted Owl. "We always do what chief say."

"There's venison sandwiches and hot coffee on the table for you," said Mrs. Bevins. "We'll see you later tonight. And again, thank you for coming."

Basil Hallstrom sat at a table in the back of the school room. He had a stack of 4 X 6 cards in front of him. He gave a card to each person as they entered.

"Print your name and affliction on the card," he instructed. "Dr. Chetham will select a few individuals who have filled out the cards to come forward."

"Will he cure my stiff hands?" asked an elderly woman.

"Dr. Chetham may be able to relieve the stiffness in your hands," said Basil. "However, please remember that some afflictions are beyond the capability of even Dr. Jeremiah Chetham. If he is unable to cure you, I am truly sorry. You can, however, pray for those unfortunate individuals he can't cure. His work is never-ending, and his travels across this great continent

107

are time-consuming and expensive. If you are able to help defray his expenses, your gift will be greatly appreciated. Your donation, with the donations of others, will enable him to visit other towns, cities, and villages across the country. Some other poor, afflicted individuals in this great land of ours will regain their health, their vitality, and their happiness because of your generous contribution."

"I'm so grateful that he has come. Let me give something now," she said, reaching into her purse.

"Oh, Madam, thank you so much," said Basil. "Your ten-dollar donation is very generous and will help Dr. Chetham immediately. I do hope he can help you."

Harold Benton leaned close to his wife and said, "He talks slicker than a big-city politician. I'm sure he'll tell everyone about her donation as they come in."

Abby watched as Basil Hallstrom passed out a card to each person entering the room. As Harold had predicted, Basil pointed to the elderly woman and told them about her ten-dollar donation.

"Now, watch, and you'll see folks reach into their pockets and make a donation before the meeting even starts," said Harold.

Abby watched for a few minutes and then leaned over to her husband. "You're right. Folks are giving him donations now. I've even seen a number of gold pieces. If this continues, he'll have hundreds, if not thousands of dollars by the end of the night."

"He has his talk down pat," whispered Harold as he stood up. "I'm going to talk to Gino. I'll be right back."

Gino stood up as Harold approached him. "The meeting room is going to be packed, Mr. Benton."

"It looks like just about everyone in town is here," said Harold. "What have you heard?"

"It is very strange. I can hear everything," whispered Gino as he pulled Harold a few feet toward the center of the meeting room. "I'm in the front of the meeting room and Basil is at the back. I don't know why, but I can hear him clearly. However, it's getting more difficult with so many people talking."

"Interesting," murmured Harold. "Thank you for the tip. I wonder how he does it."

CHAPTER 13

Saturday Evening: The buckboard creaked as it stopped in the back of the train depot warehouse. The driver set the brake, climbed down, and looped the reins around the hitching rail.

"Let's go in, Trevor," said Reverend Wesley.

"This is something I don't want to miss," said Father O'Brien, joining the reverend as they headed to the warehouse door.

"Evening, Reverend, Father," said Buckley Hodges, opening the door. "Come view the accommodations we have prepared for our guests tonight."

"That is why we came," said Father O'Brien. "Your Reverend said this was something I should see with my own eyes."

He guided them toward a small group of people and said, "First, let me introduce you to my team: Blue Bird, Forest Water, Strong Warrior, White Elk, and Dooley. Dooley is one of the Bare-X Ranch hands. Dooley will leave with you and go to the reverend's house. Forest Water and Blue Bird are experienced nurses. Strong Warrior and White Elk will help assure that our guests behave properly while they're in our care."

"Do you expect any injuries?" asked Father O'Brien, nodding toward Blue Bird and Forest Water.

110

"Blue Bird will be delivering some messages for me," said Buckley. "She also has other useful skills which I will not discuss."

"I see," said Reverend Wesley, "or should I say, I don't see."

"Iron rings are embedded in the concrete floor," said Buckley, as they walked the length of the warehouse. "They are very useful in keeping things, or people, in place."

"Very good," noted Father O'Brien.

"And here," he said, stopping in front of a large wooden box, "are shackles and handcuffs, courtesy of the railroad."

"Looks like you are ready for some uncooperative visitors."

"We hope to keep them as happy and secure as the Badger Gang members that Henry Benton brought back."

"David Acker, or should I say Rabbi Acker, told me that your son will be arriving shortly with sandwiches and coffee," said the reverend. "You should have more than enough, perhaps even some for your guests."

"I doubt that there'll be any left for our, uh, guests," laughed Mr. Hodges.

"I hear a buckboard," said Father O'Brien.

"It is Buck," said Blue Bird, looking out the door. "I know it is him because he looks like his father."

Buck climbed down from the buckboard, went to the rear, and unloaded a crate with a number of sandwiches and a large pot of coffee.

"Here's the food, Pa," said Buck. "The mugs and tea are in the next crate."

"Thank you for the delivery, son. Please thank Mr. Acker for this abundance of good food."

"I already have," said Buck, heading for the door. "I'll be right back with the other crate."

"We should be leaving for the meeting," said Reverend Wesley. "I'm pleased to see that you are ready for a multitude of guests."

"I'll be very happy if we have no guests," said Buckley Hodges. "But Brad and Audrey have a unique ability to smell trouble."

"Yes," agreed Father O'Brien, "and they predict when and where it will happen."

"We, too, hope that you have no guests," said Reverend Wesley."

The Reverend and Father O'Brien left the warehouse with Dooley. Dooley climbed in the back of the buckboard, lay down, and covered himself with a tarp. Father O'Brien climbed into the buckboard while Reverend Wesley unlooped the reins. As soon as the reverend was seated, he released the brake and slapped the reins. Gently pulling the left rein, he turned the buckboard around and headed back into town. His first stop would be his house to drop off Dooley. His second stop would be the school.

"Spotted Owl," said Trader. "I hear horse."

"Yes," said Spotted Owl. "Maybe Brad and Audrey correct."

A lone horseman came to the rear of the Bevinses' house. The two Indians watched the rider tether his horse to a tree branch, look around, and then head for the back door. Inside, Spotted Owl and Trader hid themselves in the dining room. Spotted Owl crouched behind a stuffed chair, his pistol in his hand. Trader had a coil of rawhide in his pocket and his right hand held a large knife. He stood flat against the wall beside the doorway to the kitchen.

The stranger tried the back door and found it locked. He softly cursed and kicked the door. Then, drawing his pistol, he shot the lock twice, and kicked the damaged door open. Holstering his gun, he struck a match and lit the kerosene lantern that was sitting beside the back door. Adjusting the wick, he looked around the kitchen, and stepped into the dining room.

"Do not move," ordered Trader, grasping the man's hair from behind and placing his knife on the man's throat.

"I won't," he squeaked, "Just go easy with that knife."

"I take lantern," said Spotted Owl, stepping forward as his pistol jammed into the man's stomach.

Spotted Owl took the lantern and kept his pistol poking the man's stomach as Trader tied the stranger's hands.

"What name?" demanded Spotted Owl.

"Donn Murphy," croaked the man, relieved that the knife was no longer on his throat.

"We go for ride," declared Trader.

"What are you Injuns doing here?" he demanded, trying to regain control of the situation.

"You not understand," replied Spotted Owl. "I ask what you do here. Why you shoot door? Why you break door?"

"I don't have to tell you anything," he sneered.

"Don't tell us, that okay," said Trader. "Come, we go for ride."

Trader roughly led Murphy to his horse. While Spotted Owl kept his pistol pointed at the burglar, Trader tied his hands to the saddle horn, and then tied his feet together under the belly of the horse. When he was securely tied, Trader went to the barn for their horses while Spotted Owl kept watch over the criminal.

"You can't take me!" he blustered desperately. "The Indians have a treaty with our president, the Great White Father. The soldiers, the long knives, they will free me!"

"If you talk, we tie to horse like dead man," said Spotted Owl. "How you ride?"

"I'll be quiet," he conceded.

Trader tied a long lead to Murphy's horse, then jumped on his own horse. Spotted Owl did the same, and the three of them headed to the train depot.

Walker sat by the window in the quiet, unlit house, listening to a hoot owl in the trees. Singing Coyote sat on the other side of the room, listening.

"Horse come," said Walker.

"How many?" asked Singing Coyote.

Walker listened again, and then said, "One."

Both Indians put their hands on their six-shooters, then their knives. They had left the doors unbolted.

Damon Kelly reined his horse to a halt at the hitching rail, dismounted, and looked at the house. No lanterns were lit; the house looked empty. "Hello," he called. "Anyone home?" Hearing no answer, he went up the steps and stood on the front porch. Again, he said, 'Hello, anyone home?"

Inside the unlit house, Walker and Singing Coyote lie in wait. Walker had his pistol drawn and pointed at the door. Singing Coyote stood behind the window drape, his knife ready.

Kelly grasped the door handle and turned it slowly. The door opened and he stepped inside. He struck a match, saw the kerosene lantern, lifted the glass, and lit the wick. As he was adjusting the wick, he felt a sharp object touch his back.

"Do not move," whispered Singing Coyote.

"Who are you?" he demanded.

"I Singing Coyote."

"What are you doing in my house?" snarled Damon. "You Injuns are supposed to be on your reservation."

"Guard house for Mr. Hodges," answered Walker, stepping forward, his pistol aimed at Kelly.

"Well, you better leave, and make it quick," he ordered, trying to sound authoritative. "Mr. Hodges asked me to guard his house from some renegade Injuns."

"White man lie," replied Singing Coyote. "We take to Mr. Hodges."

"Tie hands," said Walker, holstering his pistol and pulling some rawhide thongs from his pocket.

Walker quickly tied Damon Kelly's hands, blew out the lantern, and took him to his horse. Once the burglar was mounted, Walker tied the man's hands to the saddle horn, and tied his feet together under the horse's belly. Singing Coyote brought their horses from the barn, and they began their ride to Riverton.

At the Benton house, White Crow and Lone Wolf sat in the dark, just as their fellow braves had done at the Hodges' Ranch and other houses.

"Maybe bad men not come," White Crow whispered.

"Maybe not," Lone Wolf replied. "Running Bear believe little Bentons. Running Bear always right. We wait."

White Crow and Lone Wolf listened to the quiet of the night, and the occasional hoot of an owl. In the distance, they heard hoof beats. They looked at each other in the dim light and Lone Wolf gave a slow nod of his head.

Rob Hayes stopped near the oak tree, looked at the house, and hollered, "Anyone home?" The two Indians remained silent. Rob smiled and said out loud, "Since no one's home, I'm coming in." Rob led his horse to the back door and dismounted. Looping the reins over the garden fence, he placed his hand on his six-shooter, turned the knob on the back door, and entered.

In the parlor, Lone Wolf and White Crow flanked the door, their pistols drawn and aimed through the doorway into the kitchen. Hayes struck a match and lit the lantern by the back door. As he entered the parlor he felt two gun barrels jab him, one on each side.

"I take pistol," said White Crow, removing Hayes's six-shooter and sticking it in the waistband of his buckskins. "Now I take lantern," taking hold of the handle.

"Put hands in front," commanded Lone Wolf.

Hayes moved as if to follow Lone Wolf's instructions, but instead punched White Crow, pulled a knife, and slashed at Lone Wolf, cutting him across the chest. Lone Wolf reacted quickly, catching the wrist of Hayes' knife hand in a vise-like grip. White Crow, knocked back a few feet by the blow, lunged forward and struck Hayes on the side of his head with the pistol barrel.

"Ohhhh," moaned Hayes, as he dropped his knife and struggled to maintain consciousness. His wrist throbbed from the pressure of Lone Wolf's grip. He was aware of his hands being tied. He tried to kick, but his legs wouldn't respond. He felt a heavy weight pressing down on him. The room turned, he couldn't move; then everything went black.

"Lone Wolf hurt?" asked White Crow.

"Forest Water and Blue Bird fix," answered Lone Wolf. "I'll tie white man across horse."

"Yes." said White Crow. "Tie across horse, stomach in saddle."

"Him sleep because pistol hit head," said Lone Wolf. "Tie to horse now, before wake up."

So, White Crow put Hayes over his shoulder, carried him out the back door, and laid him across the saddle, stomach down. They tied his belt to the saddle with rawhide thongs, his hands to the left stirrup, and his feet to the right stirrup.

"I blowout lantern," said White Crow. "Then we go."

White Crow returned as Lone Wolf was bringing their horses from the barn. White Crow tied a lead rope to the reins of Hayes' horse and then mounted his own. They left the Benton house at a walk. At the edge of

Riverton, they turned left and took the back streets to the train depot warehouse.

Bull Bear looked at Thunder across the jail cell, "Sundown."

Thunder nodded, "Sundown."

Bull Bear reached into his pocket and pulled out the key. He walked softly to the cell door, inserted the key, turned it, and opened the door.

The cowboy in the other cell looked up in amazement, and said, "Hey, Injun, let me out too."

"Key for this door," said Bull Bear.

"Get the key from the office," urged the cowboy.

"You stay," said Bull Bear.

"Let me out or I'll holler," said the cowboy, reaching through the bars.

Bull Bear swiftly grabbed the cowboy's arm, pulling him tight against the bars. Looking intently into the man's eyes, nearly nose-to-nose, Bull Bear dropped his voice low and threatening. "Go ahead yell. Yell, I scalp; quiet, I no scalp. What you want?"

"I'll be quiet," whispered the cowboy, in a squeaky voice.

"You smart," said Bull Bear, releasing the man's arm. "You be very smart if go to church."

"Go to church?" asked the cowboy, rubbing his arms.

"Yes," said Bull Bear, as he walked into the front of the sheriff's office. "Listen to Reverend Wesley, no drink whiskey, you not be in jail. Listen to Father O'Brien, you not be in jail. If smart, you go to church."

"Maybe I will," said the cowboy, scratching his head.

"Tell Reverend you sent by friends of Running Bear," said Thunder.

Bull Bear returned from the front of the sheriff's office holding a mug of hot coffee and said, "Here coffee," offering it through the bars.

"Why, thanks," said the cowboy, taking the mug from Bull Bear. "That's right neighborly."

"Ask Sheriff Tate for church tomorrow," said Bull Bear, "Sheriff good man. He let you go."

"I think I'll do that," said the cowboy.

"Bull Bear," said Thunder. "We go now."

Bull Bear and Thunder put on their hats, checked their gun belts, and quietly left by the side door. Walking in the alley, to avoid being seen, they reached the back door of the Riverton Hotel.

"This hotel," said Bull Bear.

"Go in," said Thunder.

"Yes," said Bull Bear, his eyes glinting in the moonlight and his lips curled back in a sly smile. "Now we warriors."

CHAPTER 14

Saturday Evening: "Ladies and gentlemen." A well-dressed man spoke from the raised platform at the front of the school meeting room. "I am Dr. Jeremiah Chetham. Thank you for coming tonight. I know many of you have come here seeking a cure to your afflictions. I have healed hundreds of people in this great nation of ours. But, alas, the Lord has not given me the ability to cure all of the people that come to me. Among all who have come this evening, there are many I will not be able to cure. If you are one of the unfortunate souls whose affliction eludes my help, I am truly sorry. For those that I am able to cure, don't thank me. Thank the thousands of people that have come to my meetings and donated their hard-earned money so that I could travel to this great town of Riverton and help you. Thank those whose donations have helped me through floods, blizzards, droughts, Indian attacks, and armed desperadoes seeking personal gain."

"He's really oiling the crowd," Harold said softly in his wife's ear.

"He is a convincing orator," whispered Abby.

Dr. Chetham continued on, entrancing the crowd. Finally, he ended his speech. "Let me start the meeting by asking a lady to come forward." Dr. Chetham closed

120

his eyes, put his fingers to his forehead, and spoke slowly. "Wenda, Wenda Walker, Mrs. Wenda Walker. Will you please come forward?" Without opening his eyes, he continued. "Wenda's affliction is - her eyes."

Wenda rose from the back of the meeting room, and slowly walked down the aisle to Dr. Chetham. When she reached the platform she stopped, and looked up at him. "Yes, my eyes," she said, crying softly. "I have so much trouble seeing, even with my glasses."

Dr. Chetham knelt in front of her, removed her thick glasses, and placed his hands on her closed eyes. "Wenda, do you trust me?"

"Yes, Dr. Chetham, I trust you."

"Do you trust the Lord?"

"Yes, Dr. Chetham, I trust the Lord."

"I feel your trust," said Dr. Jeremiah Chetham. "Lord, I beg of you, feel this woman's trust. If you find her worthy, please remove the affliction that is taking her sight. Give her what only you can give, the ability to see the flowers, to see the sunrise, to see the sun set. Give her the joy of once again seeing the face of her husband."

Dr. Chetham, his eyes still closed in prayer, slowly removed his hands from Wenda's uplifted face. "Wenda, open your eyes, look at me. Can you see?"

Slowly, she opened her eyes, looked up to Dr. Chetham, to the left, and to her right, and exclaimed, "Oh, yes! I can see! I can see you!" Turning to face the people in the meeting room, she continued, "I can see like, like – like I did in my youth."

The crowd gasped in amazement at Dr. Chetham's miraculous cure. Wenda turned back to face Dr.

Chetham and sobbed, "Thank the Lord. Thank you, Dr. Chetham. Thank you for my sight. The doctors had told me I was going blind, but now I can see again. Let me help you help others," she said, reaching into her purse. Wenda pulled out a handkerchief and a leather coin purse. She wiped her eyes and blew her nose before opening the purse. She dumped the contents into her hand and said, "This is for you. Please help others."

"Thank you so much for your generous donation," said Dr. Chetham. "This will help me continue the Lord's work and help others." Looking at a woman seated in the front row, he said, "Madam, would you be so kind as to count this money and put it in the donation box? This will allow me to help more people tonight."

"Why, of course," said Mrs. Hodges, standing up and slowly walking to the donation box.

Dr. Jeremiah Chetham called up the elderly lady who had made the large donation earlier, but was unable to cure her. Facing the audience, he said, "As I said at the beginning, I can't cure everyone. For that, I am truly sorry."

As the disappointed lady returned to her seat, Harold whispered to Abby, "He got Mrs. Hodges, a local woman, to take care of the money. That makes him look more legitimate."

"It certainly does, he is a very slick man."

"And," added Harold, "I believe we can prove he is very dishonest, too."

Dr. Chetham closed his eyes, placed his fingers on his forehead, and said "Earl, Earl Walker. Earl's affliction is - is a – is a cough. Earl, please come forward."

Earl slowly came down the aisle to Dr. Chetham.

He stopped, placed a handkerchief to his mouth, and coughed a dry, hacking cough, his face reddening under the strain. After his brief coughing bout, he continued onto the platform. He stopped, and looked up at Dr. Chetham.

Dr. Chetham knelt, placed his hands on Earl's throat, and said, "Earl, are you Wenda's husband?"

"Yes," said Earl. "Didn't the Lord tell you that?"

The audience laughed, as did Dr. Chetham.

"No, he didn't. I asked the question because your last name is the same as hers. You could have been her brother."

"Oh," replied Earl.

The audience laughed again. When the laughter subsided, Dr. Chetham said, "Lord, take away the affliction that has Earl in its tenacious grip. Remove the affliction that reddens his face and leaves him gasping for air. Give Earl the thrill of speaking without coughing, to breathe freely, to walk, to run without gasping for air."

The audience watched in fascination as Dr. Chetham, with his eyes closed, looked upward, and prayed for Earl's cough. When he finished, he turned to Earl. "I don't know if you've been cured, only time will tell. How do you feel?"

"I feel, I feel great," said Earl, feeling his throat with his fingers. "I don't feel the need to cough as I have for years. You've cured me!" Turning and facing the audience, Earl again proclaimed loudly, "He cured me! He cured me!"

Wenda walked down the aisle and hugged her husband as the audience whispered to one another about what they had just witnessed. As the chatter subsided, Earl reached into his pocket, pulled out a fistful of bank notes and handed them to Mrs. Hodges, saying, "Add this to my wife's donation. Help Dr. Chetham help others. Now I'm going to take my wife to dinner and celebrate our new health."

"Harold," whispered Abby as she watched the Walkers leave the meeting room, "How does a woman earn a fistful of twenty-dollar gold pieces working as a hotel maid?"

Harold leaned over to Abby and replied, "The same way Earl earned a fistful of bank notes cleaning up the Silver Dollar Saloon."

In the front of the meeting room, Gino Donatelli quietly stood up and walked back to the Bentons. Kneeling down he spoke softly. "Harold, Basil is sending Morse code messages to Dr. Chetham."

Harold leaned toward Gino. "Morse code?"

"Yes, sir. I can hear it very clearly if I hold my head in the right position. That's how Chetham knows what's on the cards."

Gino returned to his seat at the of the room, and Harold studied Dr. Chetham intently while he worked on another man's affliction.

As soon as Gino had left, Harry Acker leaned forward and whispered, "Mr. Benton, I know how he does it."

"Does what?"

"How he hears the Morse code that his assistant sends him."

"How?"

"The sculpture behind Dr. Chetham is like the sculpture behind his assistant. They're parabolic shells. Parabolic shells amplify sound. The shells are well above the floor; thus, they avoid most of the sound from the crowd. His assistant taps the message just in front of the shell in the rear of the room. The rear shell is aimed at the shell in the front of the room. The shell in the front of the room amplifies the taps from the rear of the room enough so Dr. Chetham can hear it."

"And because it's well above the floor, we don't hear it," said Harold.

"Exactly."

"Thank you," said Harold. "Let me know what else you uncover."

"Yes sir," said Harry, quietly returning to his seat and he began examining the stage again.

Mrs. Hodges was the next person Dr. Chetham called to the stage. He prayed about her stiffness for several minutes, but to no avail; the stiffness remained.

Dr. Chetham apologized to Mrs. Hodges about not being able to help her, particularly since she was taking care of the donations. As soon as she returned to her seat, Dr. Chetham again closed his eyes, put his fingers to his forehead, and slowly said, "Gerda, Gerda Hall, Mrs. Gerda Hall. Will you please come forward?" Without opening his eyes, he continued, "Gerda's affliction is – is her arm." Gerda Hall rose from the back of the room and walked forward, stopping in front of Dr. Jeremiah Chetham.

The interior of the general store was faintly illuminated by the street lights. There was a noise at the back door, Hank Lacy and Short Bull nodded at each other. They had expected the burglars to break in from the rear and were prepared. The men outside used an iron bar to break the lock and force the door open.

"Shut the door, Willy," said a voice. "We don't want a passerby to see the open door."

Hank had his double-barreled shotgun pointed at the men, and Short Bull had his pistol drawn. Hank was partially hidden by some crates; Short Bull was behind the hinge side of the door.

"Quick," ordered Willy Brown, "strike a match and light the lantern. We'll start with the cash register and the office."

Emory Rahn struck the match and lit the lantern. He lowered the glass shade, adjusted the wick, and the two men started toward the front of the store.

"This shotgun has two barrels," said Hank, stepping into view. "I'm nervous and the triggers are light. Don't make any sudden moves."

Willy Brown slowly held up his hands. "We were just coming in from the cold. All we want is a warm place to stay for the night." Willy moved slowly to the right, away from his partner, one hand slowly moving back down towards his six-shooter.

"That's right," said Emory, moving to the left. "We just want a warm place to sleep."

Willy Brown's hand had reached his pistol, and he was preparing to draw it when Short Bull came into the light. "You not tell truth." Short Bull's pistol barrel struck Willy on the side of his head; Willy silently crumpled to the floor. Emory looked at his partner's crumpled body and quickly raised his free hand above his head.

"Now d-d-don't g-g-get nervous," stammered Emory, his voice cracking with fear. "J-J-Just tell me what you want me t-t-to do."

"Set the lantern on that crate, slowly," said Hank.

Emory did as instructed. "Just like you said," said Emory, his voice still quavering. "What now?"

"Put hands behind back," said Short Bull. "I tie hands."

"Whatever you say," said Emory, looking at his partner's crumpled form on the floor. Emory stared at Willy, his head bleeding from Short Bull's blow. He winced once as Short Bull tied his hands, but offered no resistance.

"You can sit on the floor while Short Bull gets your partner ready for a walk," said Hank, motioning with his shotgun. "You can help things out by telling us your names."

"My partner is Willy Brown," he blurted. "I'm Emory Rahn."

Short Bull gently turned Willy face down on the floor and tied his hands. Hank then handed Short Bull a pitcher of water. Short Bull slowly poured the water on Willy's head.

"Oh," groaned Willy, as he started to move.

"Your hands are tied, Willy," said Hank. "As soon as your head clears, we'll be taking a walk. In the meantime, you can tell us why you broke in. And tell the truth this time."

Emory looked at Willy's bloody head and said, "We knew the Bevinses were at the meeting, so the store would be empty."

"That's what I thought," said Hank. "I've got to

deliver a message. While I'm gone, don't talk or make any noise. My friend likes to use his knife, so don't provoke him." Short Bull walked between Willy and Emory and stood beside Hank.

"An Injun," exclaimed Emory.

"He's still collecting scalps," cautioned Hank. "I'm trying to help him break the habit. I've been successful for the most part. But when provoked, he reverts to his old ways. So, for your sake, please don't provoke him."

Hank set the shotgun down and left through the broken rear door. Short Bull carefully pulled out a long knife, and slowly walked up to Emory. He pulled up Emory's pant leg and looked at Willy, and then Emory. The two men's eyes opened wide in fear. Very purposefully, Short Bull took one slow swipe with his knife and shaved some hair off Emory's leg. Without saying a word, he pulled Emory's pant leg back down, stepped away, and returned his knife to its sheath. Short Bull, who had never scalped a man, smiled inside at the fear the two men had about being scalped.

Hank Lacy quietly entered the back of the meeting room. He waited until he caught Harry Acker's eye and nodded. Harry went to Wilma Sue Bevins and tapped her on the shoulder. She quietly got up and went to the rear of the meeting room. Hank offered her his arm and they stepped out of the door.

"Just as we expected," said Hank. "We captured two men after they broke into your store. Go get your mother."

Wilma Sue went back into the meeting room and

sat down by her mother, whispering in her ear. They got up and left the meeting room, joining Hank on the front steps.

"Evening, Mrs. Bevins," said Hank. "It's time to implement the next step of the plan."

Bull Bear and Thunder sat quietly in the Riverton Hotel's storeroom. A shaft of light entered through a small, high window that faced the back of the kitchen. On the top shelf was a crate labeled in bold letters: **Silver Services**.

"How long we wait?" asked Bull Bear.

"Until they come," said Thunder softly.

Their wait was not long. A few minutes later, the doorknob to the storeroom was slowly turned. Bull Bear and Thunder listened as a key was inserted into the lock. The click of the lock's tumblers sharpened the senses of the two Indians.

"Get the box," whispered Wenda Walker. "It's on the top shelf, labeled silver service."

"I need the ladder," her husband whispered, pulling the ladder over to the shelf. He climbed up and grasped the handles on the crate. "It feels heavy."

"It ought to be heavy," she hissed. "It's filled with silver tea services. There's thousands of dollars in that crate."

"That not yours," Bull Bear said in a low voice as he stuck his six-shooter into Wenda's back. "Tell man come down. Leave crate."

"You have to whisper a little louder," said Earl,

unaware of what was unfolding below. "I can't hear you up here."

"Come down," stuttered Wenda. "And leave the crate. I have a visitor, with a gun in my back."

"Now see here," Earl Walker pompously declared as he reached the bottom of the ladder. "Mr. Acker wants these tea services cleaned and polished by tomorrow. He'll be mighty angry with you when he finds you made us late."

"Put hands behind back," directed Bull Bear, ignoring Earl's nonsense.

Earl obeyed and Thunder quickly tied him up.

Bull Bear turned to Wenda. "Put hands in front."

Thunder tied her hands together and then tied them to her husband's hands.

"We go," announced Bull Bear, opening the door.

"Go where?" demanded Earl.

"Go for walk," Thunder said. "You want take crate. Crate not belong to you. Mr. Acker not ask you polish silver. You try steal silver."

Dr. Jeremiah Chetham was starting to call another afflicted individual when the rear door of the meeting hall opened with a crash.

"Calm down, Ma'am," said Basil Hallstrom. Calm down."

Sheriff Tate strode over to Basil, speaking forcefully. "What's all the ruckus about?"

"Our store has been robbed," cried Mrs. Bevins. "The cash register has been smashed and the money stolen. The office door is broken and the safe is gone."

Dr. Chetham saw that he had lost the audience's attention. "It must have been those Indians," he declared. "I heard that two of them are in jail."

In a matter of seconds, the room erupted in conversation. Chaos reigned supreme in the meeting hall. Dr. Chetham shouted and waved his arms to try to regain everyone's attention. His effort was in vain, as folks hollered at Mrs. Bevins, asking if anyone was hurt. While all this was going on, the sheriff tried to get everyone back into their seats. Several minutes passed before Sheriff Tate succeeded in restoring order and calming the crowd.

While Reverend Wesley and Father O'Brien had remained seated during the commotion, they had seen Dr. Chetham tie the bag of donations behind his back. When folks were in their seats again, Dr. Chetham knew it would be convincing if he prayed for the store.

"Lord," he cried out, "Deliver us from evil. Let me heal those with afflictions. Punish those who steal." He continued his prayer, successfully quieting the meeting room.

Dr. Chetham again had regained everyone's full attention. "It's time for me to call the next person," he said, closing his eyes. Before he could place his fingers on his forehead, however, Blue Bird came to the platform. "Please help me."

"How can I help you?" asked Dr. Jeremiah Chetham, opening his eyes and looking down at her.

"Please cure my affliction," said Blue Bird. "My arm was injured a year ago by Duke Badger." She held up her arm to Dr. Chetham.

"Lord," he said placing his hands on her arm, "please

heal, uh, uh, this woman's arm." Blue Bird watched him intently as he spoke.

The audience watched with great fascination. But before long, Dr. Chetham said, "I'm sorry, I cannot heal a heathen. I can only heal those who believe in the Lord."

"Dr. Chetham," said Blue Bird. "I am a Christian. Nurse Sarah Davis and Reverend Wesley brought me to the Lord."

CHAPTER 15

Nurse Sarah Davis rose from her seat, a determined look on her face. She walked up to Blue Bird and put her arm around her shoulder.

"Dr. Chetham," said Nurse Davis. "Blue Bird is not a heathen. She is a Christian. She came to your meeting at my invitation."

Blue Bird turned and faced the sheriff. "Sheriff Tate, please come forward. I have some letters for you."

The Sheriff stood up, looked at the audience, and then walked up to Blue Bird.

"Mr. Hodges asked me to deliver this to you," she said. "He said it was vital for you to read it immediately."

Sheriff Tate broke the seal on the envelope and pulled out several sheets of folded paper. He silently read the first letter silently, refolded it, and looked up at Dr. Jeremiah Chetham. "Reverend Wesley, Father O'Brien, come read this."

Reverend Wesley took the letter and unfolded it as Father O'Brien stood beside him. Together, they silently read the letter. When they finished, they both looked at the healer.

Dr. Chetham reached inside his suit coat, pulled out a pistol, and ran out the side door of the meeting room.

The meeting room was in chaos. Men stood up

shouting. Those with guns drew their weapons and headed for the side door. Those in the back of the room grabbed Basil Hallstrom, who had started to leave.

"Stay where you are!" shouted the sheriff, blocking the side door with his wide frame. "I don't want anyone getting shot. Don't chase the man. He's scared, and he'll shoot if you follow him."

Martha Wesley sat in the dark parsonage, talking with Dooley in whispers. A lone rider stopped in front of the house, then rode on. A minute later they heard another horse, this time in back of the house.

"This may be it," said Dooley.

"I have the two-shot derringer my husband gave me," said Mrs. Wesley.

"Just stay seated," said Dooley, standing up and drawing his pistol. "Don't do anything that could hurt the baby."

"I won't," replied Mrs. Wesley. "But remember, I'm your back up if you need help."

The sound of a man's boots on the back porch was quickly followed by the shaking of the doorknob. The stranger uttered a curse and then inserted a crowbar between the door and the doorjamb. The sound of tearing wood filled the kitchen. Mrs. Wesley looked at Dooley standing in the pantry, his pistol pointed at the back door.

"Finally," the stranger muttered. "Blasted doors are getting tougher to open." The stranger struck a match and lit the lantern on the kitchen wall, then turned and looked around to familiarize himself with the room.

"I hope you know how to pray," said Dooley, stepping forward.

"Who are you?" demanded the man.

"I'm the man that's placing you under arrest for burglary," said Dooley. "Now raise those hands and turn around."

"You won't shoot," asserted the man. "I can tell you're not a killer."

"But I am," said Mrs. Wesley. Martha stood in the doorway with her derringer pointed at the man. "And I won't have any qualms about killing you. Now raise those hands and turn around before I shoot."

Surprised, the man obeyed. Dooley took a pair of handcuffs from the shelf in the pantry and took a step toward the stranger.

"Now slowly, and I mean real slow," said Dooley, "Take two fingers, lift your six-shooter, and place it on the table." Again, the man did as he was ordered. He raised his hand again. "Good, now put your left hand behind your back."

"What's your name?" demanded Mrs. Wesley in a very soft voice as Dooley cuffed the man.

"Guy, Guy Rankin."

"Who's your boss?" asked Dooley.

"Boss? I don't have a boss."

"Who sent you here?" asked Dooley.

"No one."

"What made you decide to break into the reverend's house?" asked Dooley.

"I follow Dr. Jeremiah Chetham around," said Rankin. "When folks are at his meetings, I break into their houses. I wouldn't have picked this place if I'd known it was the reverend's house."

"Do you give Dr. Chetham some of what you steal?" Mrs. Wesley asked

"No way. Why should I give him anything? I do the work."

"Well, it's time to take a walk to the depot," announced Dooley, holstering his pistol and tying a rope around Guy.

"The depot?"

"That's right," said Dooley. "That's where we're taking all the burglars tonight."

"All the burglars?" Rankin asked in disbelief.

"Yes," said Dooley. "We've got men hidden in most of Riverton's houses, ranches, and businesses."

Brad, Audrey, and Mr. Acker sat in the darkened narthex of the church. "I hope we're not wasting our time," whispered Audrey. "I could be sewing my dress."

"I hope we're not wasting our time, too" whispered Mr. Acker. "I don't like to think ill of people. Most people are good."

"Shhh," whispered Brad.

The sound of creaking and breaking wood broke the stillness of the night. They watched a shaft of moonlight appear and reappear as the burglar worked on the front door. Mr. Acker drew his pistol and waited in his hiding place by the coat rack. Brad and Audrey stood in the doorway of the storeroom. Brad wiped his hands on his pant leg, firmly gripped the axe handle, and watched the door. Audrey put her hand in her coat pocket to make sure that Mr. Acker's derringer was still there.

The door finally opened, and the burglar entered, scraping his hand on the jagged edge of the broken door. "Cursed door," he snarled.

"Hold it right there," ordered Mr. Acker. "You're covered."

"That's right," said Brad, from the other side of the narthex.

"No one's taking me," he spat, lunging toward Brad.

Mr. Acker couldn't shoot because he might hit Brad. But Brad saw the large man coming and stood steady, ramming the axe handle into his stomach. There was a whoosh of air as the axe handle smashed into the charging man's stomach, stopping him where he stood. The burglar gasped for air and used the crowbar to keep his balance. Brad knocked the crowbar from the man's hands, but the burglar kept his balance as he gasped for air and tried again to hit Brad. Brad crouched down, avoiding the blow. Then with all his strength, he straightened up, extended his right arm hitting the burglar on the chin with the heel of his right hand. Blackie toppled backward like a tree hit by a bolt of lightning.

"Audrey," said Brad, breathing heavily, "Light a lantern."

"Yes," said Mr. Acker. "Let's see what Brad's done."

Audrey struck a match, lit the lantern, and adjusted the flame. She held the lantern over the man sprawled on the floor. "He looks like one of the drifters we saw come into town a few weeks ago," she said.

"How did you do that?" asked Mr. Acker. "That's a big man."

Brad described what had happened, and Mr. Acker laughed. Audrey looked at her brother in amazement. "Brad Benton, you. . . you. . . you're just like Pa!" she finally exclaimed.

"I'll tie him up while he's knocked out," said Brad. "Then I'll get the horses."

Brad quickly tied the man's hands behind his back while Mr. Acker kept his pistol pointed at the burglar. Then he unbuckled the burglars' gun belt and gave it to his sister.

"I'll get the horses and be right back," said Brad.

"Audrey, look again, closely. Are you sure he looks like one of the drifters you saw a few weeks ago?"

"Yes, Brad and I saw two men ride into town a few weeks ago, and I know this man was one of them. They were looking at the shops, especially the general store. They stopped and went into the Silver Dollar."

"We'll probably see his partner later," said Mr. Acker.

"I didn't trust him from the moment I saw him," said Audrey.

"Your instincts proved correct," said Mr. Acker.

"Sheriff Tate said I was probably right, too," said Audrey.

The clatter of horses' hooves approaching the church stopped their conversation. "That must be your brother," said Mr. Acker.

Brad stopped at the front door, looping the reins on the hitching rail and looked up at his sister and Mr. Acker. "Is he awake?" he asked.

"He's starting to come around," said Audrey, looking at the man sprawled on the floor.

The burglar tried to get up, realized his hands were tied behind his back, and started cursing.

"When I get loose, I'm gonna' make you regret you ever touched me," he shouted, struggling against his bonds.

"You can come peacefully or forcibly," said Mr. Acker. "What is your choice?"

"I'm not going anywhere with you," he shouted, struggling to his feet.

"Yes, you are," said Brad, brandishing his axe handle.

Blackie looked at Brad, and then at Mr. Acker.

"Walk, and be quiet," said Mr. Acker pointing to the steps with his pistol.

"And no more cursing," said Brad, removing a coil of rope from Ebony.

"I'll talk and curse all I want."

Brad quickly looped the rope around the man several times, and then tied it to his saddle horn. The burglar started cursing again.

"Miss Benton, may I please have your bandana?" asked Mr. Acker.

"Certainly," she said, removing it from her neck.

Taking a handkerchief from his pocket and coming up behind Blackie, Mr. Acker roughly stuffed a handkerchief in the cursing mouth and then quickly tied the bandana around Blackie's head.

"Let's go," said Brad, mounting Ebony.

"Will you ride with me, Mr. Acker?" asked Audrey, taking her foot out of her stirrup.

Mr. Acker put in his left foot and swung up behind

Audrey. "You lead, we'll follow," Mr. Acker said to Brad. "If he stops, we drag him all the way to the warehouse. The choice is his."

Brad clucked and Ebony started walking. The burglar glared at Mr. Acker, grunted, and followed. Brad rode down the center of Main Street, leading the hapless man by the rope. Mr. Acker and Audrey followed on Blaze. They halted as they reached the train depot.

"You brought us another guest," observed Dooley. "What's his name?"

"We don't know. He has trouble speaking in the presence of a lady," said Mr. Acker. "Leave the gag in until he understands your rules."

"Come on in," said Dooley. "We have quite a number of guests. Mr. Hodges would like you to take a current list of our guests to the sheriff."

Brad and Audrey looped their reins over the rail and entered the warehouse. They looked at the men and a few women who were chained to the warehouse floor.

"That's quite a number of thieves you have," said Mr. Acker, looking over the list. "Any of our people hurt?"

"One warrior got slashed with a knife," Dooley answered. "Blue Bird cleaned him up and Forest Water sewed up his shirt. The thieves have a number of wounds, mostly from getting a pistol barrel to the head."

"Here's a complete list of the ones we've captured, and the names of other gang members," said Buckley Hodges. "If you'd take this to Sheriff Tate, I'd appreciate it."

"We'll leave right away," said Audrey, taking her brother's arm.

"I'll stay here and help Buckley," Mr. Acker offered.

CHAPTER 16

The side door to the school meeting room opened, and the talking stopped. Everyone watched in complete silence as Running Bear entered, holding a pistol by its barrel.

"Dr. Jeremiah Chetham is going to join his friends," announced Running Bear, handing the pistol to Sheriff Tate.

Thank you, Running Bear," the sheriff replied. He turned to face the people in the meeting hall. "Reverend Wesley, Father O'Brien. Will you please take charge of this meeting?"

Reverend Wesley and Father O'Brien stood up and turned to face the crowd. "It will be a pleasure," said Reverend Wesley.

The Reverend spoke first. "In the Book of Matthew, Jesus touched the fevered forehead of Peter's mother-in-law and the fever left her. This cure was accomplished by faith and by a true healer, Jesus Christ."

"Also in the Book of Matthew," said Father O'Brien, "Jesus told a Roman centurion, soldier, who had great faith in the Lord that his sick servant's paralysis would be healed within the hour, and it was. He also cast the demons out of a man and into a herd of pigs. The pigs rushed into the lake and drowned. This is the power of our Lord, Jesus Christ."

The audience listened, fascinated, as the two clergymen teamed to deliver their joint sermon.

Brad and Audrey stopped at an empty hitching rail half a block away from the school and tethered their horses.

"Dr. Chetham must still be running his healing meeting," said Brad. "There are a lot of horses, wagons, and buggies around the school."

They entered the back of the meeting room and discovered Reverend Wesley and Father O'Brien talking about true faith and healing.

"We'd better get this list to the sheriff," whispered Brad to his sister.

Sheriff Tate saw Reverend Wesley looking at the back of the meeting room and turned around. Seeing Brad and Audrey, he got up and went to them.

"Dr. Chetham has been exposed," said Sheriff Tate softly. "Running Bear caught him as he ran out the back door."

"Here's a list of the prisoners in the train depot warehouse," whispered Brad, handing the sheriff a sheet of paper. "And these are Dr. Chetham's gang members that haven't been caught yet."

Their father walked over and read the list with Sheriff Tate. "I think we have just about everyone," said their father. "Brad, Audrey, I'd like you to take Victoria and your ma home. I'll be home later."

"Take my horse, Pa," Brad suggested. "I'll drive the buggy."

"Sheriff Tate," said Audrey. "You can take Blaze. Pa can bring her home.

"Thank you, Audrey, I appreciate that. I've done a lot of walking today."

"And thanks for Ebony," said her father. "It's getting late, and I don't want my family out without me. I may not get home for several hours. The sheriff needs everyone's help with the prisoners. Audrey, would you please ask Gino to join us? I'll need Gino's help, too."

"Sure, Pa."

"I think I need to tell the people how they were hoodwinked," said Sheriff Tate. "What do you think, Harold? Brad?"

"Tell them." said Harold.

"Yes," said Brad. "Tell them. After all the lies, the truth will be refreshing."

Sheriff Tate walked toward the front of the meeting room and motioned for Reverend Wesley to join him. Reverend Wesley left the preaching to Father O'Brien walked over. Sheriff Tate and the reverend talked in hushed tones for a few minutes. Reverend Wesley gave a final nod and rejoined Father O'Brien.

Father O'Brien paused. "Reverend Wesley, I believe you have something to tell the people. Am I correct?"

"Yes," said the reverend. "I'd like to tell them how Dr. Jeremiah Chetham worked his scam."

A flurry of whispers filled the hall as folks shared their theories with one another, but quickly quieted down in anticipation of the reverend's revelation.

"Ladies and Gentlemen of Riverton: It will come as no surprise after tonight's events when I tell you that Dr. Jeremiah Chetham is a thief. How he did it, however, is a journey into the depths of evil. Some simple Christian characteristics opened the door for Dr. Chetham to gain a foothold into people's lives. Those characteristics included the desire to help others and the desire to ask the Lord for help."

Reverend Wesley and Sheriff Tate explained how Basil Hallstrom had sent Dr. Jeremiah Chetham information via Morse code. Some were shocked to learn that some supposedly afflicted people were planted in Riverton weeks before Dr. Chetham arrived. Finally, the sheriff read the list of thieves who had been captured and confessed to being part of Dr. Chetham's scam. Everyone else was just plain angry about being hoodwinked and bamboozled under the guise serving the Lord. Father O'Brien and Reverend Wesley knew what to do next.

"Ladies, Gentlemen," said Reverend Wesley. "Father O'Brien and I invite all of you to one of our Easter Services tomorrow."

"I will conduct Easter Mass at eight o'clock," said Father O'Brien. "Reverend Wesley will conduct two Protestant services, one at nine-thirty and the second one at eleven. If you want to talk to us tonight, we will be here after the closing prayer."

"Let us bow our heads," said Reverend Wesley.

After the final amen, many of the people left, but quite a few came to talk to Reverend Wesley and Father O'Brien. Harold Benton and Sheriff Tate left on Ebony and Blaze, riding out to the train depot warehouse to check out the prisoners.

Brad brought the buggy to the front of the school for his mother, grandmother, and sister. When everyone was seated, Brad slapped the reins, and the four of them started their ride home. Once clear of the school, their mother proclaimed, "It seems that my two Pinkertons were right again!"

"We didn't want to be right," said Brad.

"No, we didn't," admitted Audrey. "If we hadn't seen those two drifters, we probably would have been hoodwinked with everyone else."

"And if we hadn't been tied up and robbed at the Big Foot Ranch," added Brad.

"Did you finally recognize the voice of the man who tied you up?" asked his mother.

"Yes," said Brad. "It was Earl Walker. His breath smelled of whiskey in church and at the ranch when he tied us up. His clothes always smell of whiskey."

"What was it that finally made you realize he was the man?" Nana asked.

"His confession," answered Brad. "I thought he was the one, but wasn't sure until he confessed."

"One of the men, Rob Hayes, was caught at our house," said Audrey. "Lone Wolf said nothing was broken or stolen. We were lucky."

"You said lucky. You mean some folks' homes were damaged and things were stolen?" Nana asked.

"The front door of the church was damaged, the back door of the general store, and I think the door of the Hodges' home was damaged," Audrey replied.

"Short Bull captured Gerda and Franz Hall when they drove their wagon to the back of the general store," said Brad. "Hank Lacy had come to the meeting room, and Short Bull was alone with his two prisoners. That's when Franz and Gerda arrived."

"Didn't the prisoners alert the Halls?" asked Abby.

"No," said Brad. "They were afraid that Short Bull would scalp them. As soon as the Halls entered, Short Bull knocked Franz out and held his knife to Gerda's throat."

"Short Bull threatened her with a knife?" Nana exclaimed. "Why, he's such a gentle and loving man. You should see him play with his children. I don't think he could hurt anyone."

"That may be true," said Audrey. "But he certainly scared his prisoners. It's a good thing he scared them, too. Gerda let him tie her up without any fussing, either. The two prisoners told her that he still scalped people if they crossed him."

"Short Bull, why he's never scalped anyone," admonished Nana. "Just ask Running Bear."

"Mr. Lacy told the prisoners that Short Bull still scalped folks when he's provoked," said Brad.

"Why that little fibber," laughed Nana. "The next time I see him I'm going to tell him he's not supposed to fib, unless, of course, he fibs to thieves about getting scalped if they don't cooperate. Those fibs are just fine."

"I'm glad no one got seriously hurt," said their mother. "Blue Bird said that Lone Wolf's knife cut was shallow, nothing to be concerned about. She cleaned it and put some ointment on it."

"I'll wait up for Harold," said Nana. "I took a nap this afternoon, so I'm rested."

"Tomorrow will be busy," said their mother. "Reverend Wesley is conducting two Easter services."

"That means we'll be baby-sitting for two services," said Audrey. "We won't get home until early afternoon."

"I'll have a nice Easter dinner ready when you return. Your pa and I will come back after the nine-thirty service. He'll come back for your ma a little after twelve."

"When we get home, I'm heading to bed," said Brad, stifling a yawn. "Pa can tell us about the prisoners in the morning. I wonder if there's a reward for any of them."

CHAPTER 17

Easter Sunday, 18 April 1881: Brad stopped the buggy at the front of the church. The damaged door reminded him of Blackie Harrington and the events of last night. His father helped their mother, Nana, and Audrey down while Brad kept his foot on the brake and held the reins.

"Reverend Wesley will announce what Sheriff Tate told him about Dr. Chetham's gang," said their father. "That should answer some of the questions you had this morning."

"I'm sure it will," said Brad, as he released the brake and slapped the reins. "Save a seat for me." Brad parked the buggy behind the church under a large tree. As he tied the horse to the hitching rail, he watched the other buggies, wagons, and buckboards converging at the church.

"The church will be packed this morning," predicted Audrey as Brad sat down beside her. "Easter Sunday and the exposure of Dr. Chetham last night will bring most of the town folks out."

"I'm anxious to hear what Reverend Wesley has to say," said Brad. "But I'm also ready for my favorite Easter Hymn, 'Jesus Christ is Risen Today'."

148

"That's one of my favorites, too," said Audrey. "What did Nana tell you about it?"

"She said the hymn, the text, and the music, date from the late 1400s. Charles Wesley, an Anglican priest, smoothed out the melody and titled the revised hymn, calling it 'Salisbury.'"

"Wasn't Charles Wesley John Wesley's brother, the founder of the Methodist Episcopal Church?" Audrey asked.

"One and the same. But Charles remained a priest in the Church of England. He didn't become a Methodist," said Brad. "But he did write a lot of hymns, over 6,000 I believe, many of them for his brother."

"Ma's getting ready for the opening hymn," Audrey noticed. "Tell me more later."

As their mother played the introduction, Reverend Wesley stayed in the back of the church singing,

Jesus Christ is ris'n today. Alleluia!
Our Triumphant holy day, Alleluia!
Who did once upon the cross, Alleluia!
Suffer to redeem our loss. Alleluia!

As the fourth verse began, Reverend Wesley strode down the aisle singing and took his seat beside the pulpit. The deacons read the scriptures, and the reverend gave his Easter Sermon. The church was packed. Little children sat on their mother's and father's laps. Some of the latecomers had to stand behind the last row of pews or in the narthex during the service because every pew was full.

"The shortage of seats has forced many folks to

stand, so I'll keep my announcements brief," said the reverend. Heads nodded in agreement, and folks in the front pews turned around and saw that the church was packed.

"Dr. Jeremiah Chetham is a fake, and a fraud," said the reverend. "He is not a healer. He is not a preacher. He is a thief."

Some folks nodded in agreement, some looked knowingly at their neighbors, and the few who hadn't yet heard about the exposure of Dr. Jeremiah Chetham gasped in amazement. Reverend Wesley continued. "We captured twelve members of Chetham's gang last night, and one man who followed Chetham, but wasn't a member of his gang."

There were 'ohs' and 'ahs' from those who found the news hard to believe. Those who already knew about the gang's capture nodded in agreement.

"We recovered the money that was donated last night but haven't found any of the valuables that were stolen from homes during the past few weeks. When, or if, the valuables are recovered, Sheriff Tate will do everything he can to notify the rightful owners." Reverend Wesley nodded to Abby, and she began playing the Offertory.

Jake Jackson had to borrow Buckley Hodges' hat because the offering plate got too full to hold any more. Jake presented the offering plate and the hat to a deacon. At the end of the service, just before the final hymn, Reverend Wesley announced that Buckley would have to stay after church to get his hat back.

Wilma Sue met Brad and Audrey at the bottom of the church steps. "We caught thirteen outlaws last night!" exclaimed Wilma Sue, "Thirteen!"

"And no one was seriously hurt, either." Brad smiled.

"We were fortunate that Running Bear was able to get so many of his braves to help," said Audrey. "We'll have to finish sharing stories at school tomorrow. I see your Pa bringing the buckboard up now."

"Aren't you going home?" asked Wilma Sue.

"No," said Audrey. "Ma has to play at the second service, and Pa is going to meet with Sheriff Tate. We're going to stay and help take care of the little kids during the next service. This is one of the few times in the year that Reverend Wesley has somebody watch the children, if the parents want to have someone watch them."

"See you Monday," said Wilma Sue, as her father stopped the buckboard.

CHAPTER 18

Friday, 23 April 1881: "Audrey," said Miss Jones, looking at a note that just been handed to her. "Would you please step into the hall with me for a moment?"

Audrey looked at Brad, confused. "Yes, Ma'am."

Audrey followed Miss Jones into the hall, wondering what had happened. Had she done something wrong? Was their mother or father hurt? No, or Brad would have been called into the hall with her. Well, she thought, *I'll know in a moment.*

"Father O'Brien just had this note delivered to the school," said Miss Jones. "Mrs. Wesley is in labor, and Nurse Davis needs your help because Doc Adams is out of town."

Audrey smiled and said, "Doc Adams explained everything to me when we examined Mrs. Wesley a few weeks ago. He said I should know what to do if he or Nurse Davis were not available. But I never thought I'd be helping deliver a baby."

"The school day is almost over," said Miss Jones. "Why don't you leave now? Will Brad take your books home for you?"

"Of course he will," said Audrey quickly. Then she put her hand to her mouth and said, "I believe he will, but I'd better ask him."

152

Miss Jones opened the door and said, "Brad, will you come here for a moment?"

"Yes, Ma'am," replied Brad.

When Brad was in the hall, Miss Jones closed the door, and Audrey said, "Will you take my books home for me? Mrs. Wesley is in labor, and Nurse Davis needs my help."

A smile spread across his face as he realized what was happening. "Of course, and I'll come back with our horses and keep the fire hot and anything else I can do to help. You go help with the baby."

"Audrey, you can leave now," said Miss Jones. "Let me know about the delivery on Sunday."

Audrey quickly put on her coat, left the school, and ran to Reverend Wesley's house. Panting, opened the gate and tried to catch her breath as she walked to the front porch. Raising her hand to knock, she paused briefly, listening. She heard a woman's voice, but couldn't understand what was being said. She knocked.

"Is that you, Audrey?" called Nurse Davis.

"Yes."

"Come in, we're in the bedroom."

Audrey opened the door and went to the bedroom. Mrs. Wesley was in the bed; her face was wet and pale. Before Audrey could say anything, Mrs. Wesley grimaced as another contraction started.

"The baby will be coming in in a matter of hours," said Nurse Davis. "Can you heat some water?"

"Of course," replied Audrey as she headed to the kitchen. "Brad will be coming after school; he'll help too."

"We could certainly use an extra pair of hands by then."

Audrey took the last piece of wood from the woodbox and put it in the stove. She thought about the birthing process that Doc Adams had explained to her as she pumped the kettle full of water. The wet kettle bottom hissed as she set it on the stove.

"The water's heating," said Audrey, coming back into the bedroom.

"Good," said Nurse Davis. "Now I'd like you to stand by Martha and press on the small of her back each time she has a contraction. That will ease the strain on her back and make the delivery easier."

"Where's Reverend Wesley?" asked Audrey.

"He left this morning with Doc Adams," answered Mrs. Wesley, "They drove out to the Johnsons, a new family about an hour out of town. That was just before my labor started. They'll be back around dark."

"And Father O'Brien? He had a note delivered to the school asking me to help you."

"He'll be in and out," said Nurse Davis. "He's working with Sheriff Tate; they're writing letters and sending telegrams about Dr. Chetham and his gang."

"He said there might be rewards on some of the gang members," said Audrey.

"The best reward," said Mrs. Wesley, "is. . . ohhh. . . ohhh." She stopped talking as another contraction started. Audrey pressed on Mrs. Wesley's back, and Nurse Davis held the mother's hand as the contraction strengthened.

"Nana!" shouted Brad, running into the house. "Mrs.

Wesley is having the baby. Audrey is at her house helping Nurse Davis."

"That's wonderful!" said Nana. "They're looking forward to the child."

"I've got to take some clothes for Audrey. She might have to stay overnight. I've got to keep the water hot and help Nurse Davis. I'm going to saddle the horses and leave right away."

"I'll pack some sandwiches for all of you. I'll have them ready by the time you finish saddling the horses."

"Thanks, Nana, I'll be right back."

Brad grabbed a couple of carrots from the root cellar and ran to the barn.

"Got to hurry, Ebony. You too, Blaze, here's your carrot."

In just a few minutes, Brad had the horses saddled and bridled. He led them out of the corral and tied them to the hitching rail.

I've got to hurry he said to himself, running to the back door.

"Here's sandwiches, cookies, and apples for supper," said Nana, opening the door. "Stay as long as you're needed."

"Thanks, Nana," he said as he put the food into his saddlebag.

Brad mounted, gave a tug on Blaze's lead, and clucked Ebony to a lope.

As he reached Riverton he slowed the horses to a fast walk. When they reached the reverend's house, Blaze instinctively stopped at the hitching rail with Ebony. Brad looped the reins around the rail, ran to the front porch, and knocked.

Nurse Davis opened the front door and said. "Brad Benton, you arrived just in time. Martha's in labor and we're just about out of wood."

"I'll get right at it," he said, following her into the house. He opened the kitchen stove, looked in at the fire and then at the empty woodbox. "The fire is low," he said to himself. "I'd better get chopping."

"Ohhhhhh," groaned Mrs. Wesley as another contraction started. Audrey pressed on Mrs. Wesley's back while Sarah held her hand and encouraged her to bear down.

Before long Brad had chopped an armload of wood. He dumped it in the kitchen woodbox and put a few pieces in the stove. He watched as the new wood start smoking and then caught fire. He closed the lid of the stove, looked around the kitchen, and went to the bedroom door.

"I filled the woodbox and put some more wood in the stove," said Brad. "Would you like some tea?"

"Yes," said Nurse Davis. "I haven't eaten since . . . since this morning."

"Nana made some sandwiches," said Brad. "They're in my saddlebags. I'll let you know when dinner is ready."

Brad went down the steps and stopped in front of Blaze and Ebony. "I brought an apple for each of you," he said reaching into his saddlebags. Ebony nickered as he offered her an apple. Blaze nuzzled his arm. "I have one for you, too, girl," said Brad, giving her the other apple.

Brad set the sack of food on the counter. He rinsed his hands and face at the kitchen pump. Opening the cabinets, he found plates and set the table for three, putting one of Nana's sandwiches on each plate.

"Dinner is served, m'ladies," announced Brad, a towel draped across his right forearm, imitating an English butler.

"We'll come as soon as the next contraction is over," said Nurse.

As soon as they were seated, Brad said a short blessing and they began eating.

"Audrey told me that you make good tea," said Nurse, setting her mug down. "She was right. And I must thank your grandmother for the sandwiches, too."

"How long before the baby comes?" asked Brad.

"Within the next few hours," explained the nurse. "It could even be in the next few minutes. When the baby is ready, he'll come."

"It's a boy?" asked Audrey.

"I don't know," said the nurse. "We just refer to the babies as boys until they're born."

"Just like horses are called girls until you know if they're a stallion," commented Audrey.

"And speaking of horses," said Nurse Davis. "Martha will be hungry as a horse after she delivers. I really can't give her anything to eat now, her stomach can't handle it."

Nurse Davis and Audrey left the table several times during the meal to help Mrs. Wesley. After they had finished eating their sandwiches, Nurse Davis explained the birthing process again.

"Another contraction is starting," panted Mrs. Wesley from the bedroom.

"She just finished one. They're getting closer

together," remarked the nurse, getting up from the table. "We're getting close to delivery."

Quite a few contractions later, Nurse Davis said, "Brad, bring me a basin of hot water, but not so hot I can't put my hands in it."

Brad poured the water from the kettle into the basin, and then slowly pumped water from the well until it was cool enough for his hands.

"Here's the water," he said, setting the basin on the chair by the bed.

"The baby's head is coming," she Sarah. "It's just about over, Martha. When the next contraction starts, give it all you've got."

When the next contraction began, Audrey held Mrs. Wesley's hands as Nurse Davis helped the baby.

"The head is out," she said. "Give me another push."

"I'm so tired," whispered Mrs. Wesley.

"You're almost through. Just one, maybe two more pushes," she encouraged, as the next contraction started. "Good, the shoulders are free. Keep going, you're almost done."

A minute later the baby cried. "Martha, you have a baby boy!" Nurse Davis exclaimed.

As she cleaned the baby's mouth, she said, "Audrey, dip one of the towels in that basin of warm water."

As Audrey worked, Nurse Davis tied and cut the umbilical cord.

"How is the baby?" Mrs. Wesley asked weakly.

"He looks beautiful. Ten fingers, ten toes, one nose, two eyes, two ears."

"I didn't mean that," laughed Mrs. Wesley. "Is he healthy?"

"Absolutely, but don't expect him to start preaching like his father, at least not for a few years."

"Here it is," said Audrey, handing the warm towel to Nurse Davis. "The baby is looking around."

"Yes, some do that as soon as they're born. Some cry until they're in their mother's arms. Every baby is different. Each has their own personality. I'll need another wet towel," one is never enough. Then I'll need a dry towel."

After giving her another wet towel, Audrey began cleaning up the afterbirth and helped making Mrs. Wesley more comfortable.

"You won't want to eat right away," explained the nurse. "But, while you're holding the baby I'll start fixing you a real meal. How about bacon, scrambled eggs, and toast with blueberry jam?"

"My stomach is starting to feel better," said Mrs. Wesley. "Maybe I'll be hungry in half an hour, but not now."

"Here he is," said Nurse Davis, placing the infant, now wrapped in a soft flannel blanket, in Mrs. Wesley's arms. "He needs to be held and kept warm. Being born is as hard on the baby as it is on the mother."

"The dishes are washed and dried," said Brad, standing at the bedroom door.

"Come in, Brad," said Mrs. Wesley. "Meet my son."

"Have you and Bob selected some names?" asked Nurse Davis as Brad came over to the side of the bed.

"Yes, but he wants to announce the baby's name at church. He'll also want to announce the birth on Sunday, so don't tell anyone."

Audrey look at Nurse Davis. "How did you train be a nurse?"

"I was fortunate; I had an uncle who bequeathed a large sum to a nursing school with the stipulation that they train me. I was trained, and now here I am."

"That was a nice, short story," said Mrs. Wesley. "Now how about the long version?"

"Well, as I said, my uncle bequeathed a large sum of money to the Belview Nursing School in New York. I was in the first class when the school started in 1873."

Nurse Davis continued, providing greater detail about her training as a nurse, her capture by Duke Badger, and finally, her rescue by Henry Benton.

"I'm ready for that dinner you described," said Mrs. Wesley. "I'm ravenously hungry."

"I'll start it right away."

"I'll help," said Audrey.

The bacon was sizzling in the frying pan when they heard a buggy stop in front of the house. The front door opened and Reverend Wesley and Doc Adams entered the house.

"Sarah," greeted Reverend Wesley. "I didn't expect to see you here." Seeing Audrey and Brad he continued. "I didn't expect to see two Pinkertons in my house, either. The sheriff is still sending wires about Dr. Jeremiah Chetham; he doesn't have time for another case. Any new outlaws will just have to wait."

"Well," remarked Nurse Davis. "You have to make time for the newest case; we're calling it 'The Case of the New Baby.' Congratulations! Martha had a baby boy about half an hour ago."

"A boy!" exclaimed the reverend. "How is Martha?"

"Martha is fine," said Sarah, "and so is the baby. I'm fixing her dinner now, bacon and eggs."

"I'll give her a quick exam," said Doc Adams, "any problems?"

"Nothing unusual; Audrey helped me with the delivery, and Brad kept us supplied with hot water and food. But please confirm that everything is fine."

"I'll do that. Audrey, come help me while Nurse Davis fixes dinner for the new mother. Bob, I'll need you, too, to hold the baby."

"I think I can handle that," said the reverend, a big smile on his face.

Doc Adams examined the baby, explaining to Audrey what he was doing as he proceeded. When he finished, he handed the baby to Bob. The doctor's exam of Mrs. Wesley was more detailed as he explained to Audrey what he was checking for and why. He was just finishing when Sarah appeared at the bedroom door with a platter of food.

"Your patient is going to die of hunger," she said. "I've brought the medicine that always works: A big meal."

"She needs that medicine, too," laughed the doctor. Everything is fine, Sara, just as you described. I'm going home; Rosemary has my dinner waiting. I'll see you later."

"We should be getting home too," said Brad.

"Yes," Audrey agreed as she looked out the window. "It's getting dark."

"Thanks for your help," said the reverend. "This was a surprise! We didn't expect the baby for another week."

"Glad we could help," said Audrey.

"We'll see you Sunday," added Brad, closing the front door.

Ebony nickered as they came down the steps. Brad un-looped the reins and they mounted their horses.

"Let's go," said Brad, gently nudging Ebony's flanks.

The horses walked until they reached the edge of town, then broke into a trot the rest of the way home. It was after sunset by the time they reached the house. Brad dismounted and opened the corral gate. The horses went directly into the barn.

"I'll get the lantern," said Audrey, entering the dark barn. The light of the moon illuminated the tack room just enough so that Audrey could see the shape of the lantern and the small metal box on the shelf below it. Retrieving a match, she struck it and lit the wick.

"The Case of the New Baby," said Brad, taking off Blaze's saddle. "Sounds like something a Chicago detective would say."

"We have helped capture quite a few outlaws," said Audrey, putting a scoop of oats into Ebony's feed trough.

"You're right," said Brad. "But we don't go looking for thieves. Thieves, well, they, uh...."

"They seem to find us."

"That's right. The Badger Gang took Pa, and Duke Badger's son came to Riverton."

"I know," said Audrey, blowing out the lantern. "Dr. Jeremiah Chetham came to Riverton, and one of his men robbed our house."

"And Franz Hall tied us up when we went to the Big Foot Ranch," said Brad, as they walked to the back door.

"But we did track the Big Foot Gang."

"True, but they captured Running Bear while we were waiting for you to bring the sheriff."

Brad and Audrey entered the kitchen and smelled cinnamon. Their grandmother was standing in the doorway to the parlor.

"Welcome back," she said. "Was it a boy or a girl? Is Mrs. Wesley all right?"

"She and the baby are both fine," reported Audrey. "Nurse Davis did everything that Doc Adams told me to do."

"It's a boy," added Brad. "Reverend Wesley will announce the baby's name at church this Sunday. We're supposed to keep quiet about it until then."

"Thanks for sending the sandwiches and cookies with Brad," said Audrey. "We ate supper a few bites at a time between Mrs. Wesley's labor pains."

"The sandwiches were nice," said Brad, loudly sniffing the aroma of the hot cinnamon again. "But they weren't as filling as one of your meals."

"Oatmeal cookies are ready," said Nana, smiling at her grandson. "There's no need for you to wear out your nose, and the tea kettle is always ready. Wash up, get some cookies, and tell us all about it. I'll get your parents; they'll want to hear, too."

Brad and Audrey started with the note at school and finished with Doc Adams and Reverend Wesley returning home.

"Doc Adams checked Mrs. Wesley and said she was fine?" questioned their grandmother.

Brad finished his second large cookie, "Yes, he did, that's when we came home."

"It's late, and I expect both of you are tired," said their mother.

"I am ready for bed," declared Brad.

"Me, too," echoed his sister.

"Hustle yourselves upstairs," instructed their mother. "We've got lots of errands and chores to do tomorrow; I need the two of you well rested.

"Good night," said Brad.

"Good night," said Audrey, following her brother up the stairs to her room.

"So," said Brad, "you're thinking about becoming a nurse."

"How did you know?" asked Audrey.

"You really took an interest in everything Doc Adams and Nurse Davis did. Your skill in helping Mrs. Wesley is unique. Nurse Davis told me you did as well as Doc Adams. If you want to become a nurse, do it."

"But the training that she described costs a lot of money," said Audrey.

"And we have a lot of money in the bank from capturing outlaws," said Brad. "Good night. I'll see you in the morning."

Brad gently closed his door. Audrey looked at the closed door and listened to her brother take off his boots and get ready for bed.

Maybe I can become a nurse, she thought going into her room.

CHAPTER 19

Sunday, 25 April 1881: It was sunny and calm with a few white puffy clouds in the sky as Brad and Audrey stopped in front of the sheriff's office. They looped their reins over the hitching rail and stepped up on the boardwalk.

"Pa said that most of the stolen items were found," said Brad as he opened the door.

"Morning, Brad, Audrey," greeted Sheriff Tate. "Thanks again for your help in capturing Dr. Chetham and his gang. I suppose you came to claim your rifle and your Ma's locket."

"That's right," replied Audrey. "What else did you recover?"

"Quite a bit. The Halls' wagon had a false bottom. When we opened it, we found four rifles, one shotgun, five pistols, some jewelry, and some money. That included Brad's rifle and your Ma's locket."

"Then you found Mr. Lacy's rifle and pistol, too," said Brad.

"We did. We also recovered $2,570, most of it from the meeting. Since Mrs. Hodges handled the donations, we should be able to return the money to the folks that donated it."

"What about the gangs' wagon, horses, and weapons?" asked Audrey.

"The horses will be sold at the livery," said the sheriff. "Buckley Hodges will sell the guns. The money we receive from the guns and horses will pay for the doors and windows the gang broke. Any money left over after the bills are paid will go to the town of Riverton."

"When can we take Brad's rifle and Ma's locket?" asked Audrey.

"As soon as you sign for them, you can have them." The sheriff pushed a piece of paper and pen across his desk.

"I'll sign for my rifle now," said Brad, dipping the pen in the inkwell.

"And I'll sign for Ma's locket," said Audrey, caressing her mother's keepsake. "Then we've got to leave for church."

"And I'll be picking up Miss Jones, your teacher, in a few minutes," said the sheriff. "I trust the reverend will have a good sermon for us."

Brad and Audrey dismounted and tied their horses to the church hitching rail.

"I see the Bevinses' buggy," said Brad.

"And Harry is coming, too," added Audrey.

"Morning, Brad, Audrey," said Wilma Sue, "and Harry," she added.

"Morning, everyone," said Harry. "I see the Hodges' buckboard at the corner now. It looks like we're all going to be here."

"I still can't believe we all helped capture Dr. Chetham's gang," marveled Wilma sue.

"We needed help from a lot of people," said Brad.

"How many people helped?" asked Wilma Sue. "Trader and Spotted Owl were at our house, and Short Bull was at our store with Hank Lacy."

Brad thought for a moment. "Running Bear had thirteen braves from his village, and then there was Hank, Zeke, Dooley, Blue Bird, Mr. Hodges, and," closing one eye as he thought, "I think that was it."

"That was nineteen people," said Audrey. "And Mr. Acker makes twenty."

"The two of you makes twenty-two," said Harry. "And when you add the rest of us, that makes twenty-five."

"How many gang members did we finally catch?" asked Wilma Sue.

"Ma's starting the prelude," said Audrey. "We'd better get seated."

"If I know Reverend Wesley," said Brad as they entered the church, "he'll tell us about the gang, and something else."

"Something wonderful," Audrey whispered to Wilma Sue.

"What's that?" she whispered excitedly, hanging to Audrey's arm.

"You'll find out!" Audrey winked as she entered her pew.

"What is it?" Wilma Sue whispered again as Mrs. Benton played the introduction to the hymn.

"You'll find out!" she mouthed and then joined in as the congregation began singing the first verse.

Reverend Wesley's sermon on faith was appropriate.

Dr. Jeremiah Chetham's gang had been picked up by sheriffs and Colorado's U.S. Marshal. Dr. Chetham, however, had the distinction of having two policemen come all the way from Chicago for him.

When Reverend Wesley came down to the front pew with several sheets of paper in his hand and started making announcements, folks knew they had better pay attention. The last time he had had a sheet of paper in his hand the announcements were better than his sermon, and his sermons were always good.

"I'll start with this telegram from Sheriff Strong in Denver. There are rewards for three members of the Healer Gang, or what Rabbi Acker calls the Passover Bandits. Sheriff Strong sent two deputies earlier this week and took the criminals back to Denver. Blackie Harrington: Wanted for robbery and murder, a reward of $2,000. Willie Brown: Wanted for robbery, a reward of $1,000. Emory Rahn: Wanted for robbery, a reward of $1,000.

The congregation nodded in approval. After all, their Reverend had helped plan the capture of the gang.

The Reverend continued, "I also have a telegram from Chicago. There is a reward for Dr. Jeremiah Chetham. It seems that he tricked many citizens of Chicago with his fake healing. Before I tell you any more about Dr. Chetham, I want to remind you about greed and faith. Rule number one: If it sounds too good to be true, it probably isn't true. Rule number two: If you have to give someone your valuables to get faith, it isn't faith, it's fakery."

The reverend concluded, "Faith in the Lord makes life so much easier; faith that his son died for our sins, faith that must be kept in spite of our wounds, our injuries, and our afflictions. When Saint Peter asks if you experienced wounds, afflictions, pain, and suffering, he expects you to say 'Yes, I experienced pain, I experienced afflictions, and I experienced wounds. I suffered in the service of my Lord.'"

There was a murmur of acknowledgment in the congregation. Then the reverend said, "I'm starting a sermon; I'd better stop." The congregation laughed, and folks looked at each other and nodded in agreement.

"Coming back to Dr. Jeremiah Chetham," said the reverend, "The reward for him is sizeable. Detective Pulaski will be coming next week from Chicago with more details. I have faith that the reward will pay for our high school teacher and books for several years.

The congregation was excited by this news, whispering amongst themselves.

"Now for my final announcement. I swore Doc Adams, Nurse Davis, Brad and Audrey Benton, and Father O'Brien to secrecy, Miss Jones, too."

The congregation sat up straight and scooted to the edge of their seats. He had already made some mighty powerful announcements. This next one had to be a real whopper.

"Friday night, I became the father of a baby boy, Robert Bradley Wesley. Martha and the baby are doing fine. I'd like to thank Audrey Benton for helping Nurse Davis in the delivery. Sarah, Audrey, please stand up."

Audrey stood up, her red face glowing just about as bright as her blond hair in the morning sun. Sarah, standing behind her, leaned forward and put her hand on Audrey's shoulder. The congregation applauded with joy. Then Audrey sat down, her face still red.

"Abby, the closing hymn, please," said the reverend.

Mrs. Benton played the introduction, and the reverend's powerful voice encouraged his flock to sing enthusiastically, which was easy after the announcements they had just heard.

The congregation lined up to leave the church, talking to the reverend on their way out. Wilma Sue threaded her way through the aisle to the Bentons.

"Audrey Benton," she Wilma Sue. "Why didn't you tell me you had helped deliver the baby?"

"The reverend swore her to secrecy," Nurse Davis interjected. "She couldn't tell you."

"Well, you could have told me, and that it was a secret," pleaded Wilma Sue. "I wouldn't have told anyone about the baby. At least I don't think would have told anyone."

The citizens of Riverton patted each other on the back and congratulated the reverend on the announcements and new baby. And, oh yes, the sermon was good too.

While their parents talked to each other, Wilma Sue, Brad, Audrey, Buck, and Harry met under a tree in front of the church. Harry immediately asked, "Who is Riverton getting to come teach the high school students next year?"

"My Pa has been sending letters and telegrams for several weeks," said Buck. "He said few teachers have expressed a willingness to come to Riverton. Most don't want to come; they want to stay close to their homes. They can make more money there, too. It's not easy getting teachers to come out west."

"My father is helping too," said Harry. "He said he thinks they have found the perfect teacher, but he won't tell me about him or her."

"Pa's waving to me," said Wilma Sue. "I've got to go."

"My family is waiting, too," said Buck. "I'll see you in school tomorrow."

"Until tomorrow then," said Brad. "Let us know if your father says anything else about the high school teacher."

"I will!" said Harry.

Brad and Audrey mounted their horses and followed their parents' buggy home.

CHAPTER 20

Sunday, 2 May 1881: Father O'Brien stood in the church doorway and looked at the town of Riverton. He had just said goodbye to the Donatellis, the last family of his parish to leave after Sunday Mass. A man wearing a suit, bowler hat, and a gun belt, walked toward the church. He was a stranger to Riverton. *Probably just passing through*, thought Father O'Brien.

"Morning," said Father O'Brien. "Our Catholic service finished a few minutes ago. Reverend Wesley's Protestant service begins at ten o'clock."

"You must be Father O'Brien," said the stranger. "I need to talk to you and Reverend Wesley." The man paused. "Excuse me, I should have introduced myself. I'm Jedrik Pulaski, Detective Jedrik Pulaski, of the Chicago Police Department."

"I heard you were coming," said Father O'Brien. "I understand you were looking for one of our jail guests, Dr. Jeremiah Chetham. Am I correct?"

"For the most part," said the detective, a smile slowly spreading across his face. "I also came on behalf of the senior priest of my parish, Saint Mary's of Chicago."

"I see buggies and horses coming for Reverend Wesley's service; let's move inside where we can talk with a little more privacy."

172

"Whatever you say," he said, following Father O'Brien into the church.

"I wonder who that is talking to Father O'Brien," said Brad as he and his sister stopped at the hitching rail.

"We may have to wait a while to find out," replied Audrey. They're going into the church."

"There are the Bevinses. Wilma Sue may have heard something at the store yesterday."

"Morning, Brad, Audrey," greeted Wilma Sue. "Who was Father O'Brien talking to?"

"That's just what we were going to ask you," said Brad.

They were exchanging theories about the stranger when Buck joined them. Buck waited until his parents entered the church, then quickly changed the subject.

"I heard my Pa talking with Ma last night," said Buck. "They have a high school teacher for next year."

"What's his name?" asked Brad.

"Or," interjected Audrey, "what's her name?"

"All I heard was the name Megan," said Buck. "So I expect it's a lady."

"I hear the prelude," said Audrey. "We've got to go."

"I'm going to try to talk with Father O'Brien," said Brad. "Keep the pew warm."

Brad stopped in the narthex, trying to catch the priest's eye. When the prelude was over, Brad knew he had to join his family. He reached Audrey just as his mother was finishing the introduction to the hymn.

"Well?" asked his sister.

"I heard them say 'high school teacher' a few times," whispered Brad. "They were talking with Reverend Wesley just before the opening hymn, too."

Reverend Wesley's strong voice filled the building

from the back of the church as the congregation sang the first verse of the opening hymn. Reverend Wesley's sermon was on patience and giving thanks. Everyone in Riverton knew Father O'Brien, but they were a little surprised to see a Catholic priest and a stranger sitting together in the front pew during Reverend Wesley's Protestant service.

Reverend Wesley stepped from the pulpit and strode purposefully down the center aisle, stopping just short of the first row of pews.

"Good morning," he said, to which the congregation responded with a vibrant "good morning."

"I saw enough stares and heard enough whispers in the congregation this morning to know that everyone is curious about the gentleman in the front pew with Father O'Brien. Detective Pulaski, please stand up. The floor is yours."

"Thank you, Reverend Wesley. Before the service Father O'Brien asked me to join him and all of you at your Protestant service to make an announcement. He warned me, however, that even though Reverend Wesley delivers good sermons, I must remain a Catholic."

The congregation laughed at the detective's candor. After the capture of Dr. Jeremiah Chetham and his gang, the congregation knew Father O'Brien and Reverend Wesley were united in their effort to win souls. They knew their religious leaders were not competing but collaborating for souls.

"There is a sizeable reward for Dr. Jeremiah Chetham," said the detective. "His real name, however, is Jerry Chetham. He's been tricking good Christian folks, like you out of money for over six years. He'll have a trial, and if convicted, be spending many years behind bars in an Illinois prison. The City of Chicago and the State of Illinois posted a reward for his capture. I'm presenting a bank draft in the amount of $3,000 payable to Father Trevor O'Brien and Reverend Robert Wesley. Thank you for capturing this wicked man."

Detective Pulaski shook hands with Reverend Wesley and Father O'Brien as the congregation applauded. When the applause subsided, he said, "Father O'Brien told me that Buckley Hodges is in the congregation."

Buckley stood up. "I certainly am."

"Would you please come forward? I have a letter that I was asked to hand-deliver to you."

Mr. Hodges came to the front of the church. Detective Pulaski handed him a sealed envelope.

"Father Ogroski, the senior priest at Saint Mary's, requested that you read the letter to yourself, and then if you concur, to the congregation."

Mr. Hodges read the letter to himself as the congregation sat in such total silence that all they could hear was the chirping of blue birds outdoors. Mr. Hodges smiled, refolded the letter, and handed it to Father O'Brien.

"Father," said Mr. Hodges. "If you don't mind, I'd like to make the announcement."

Father O'Brien read the letter, smiled, and said, "By all means, please do."

"A teacher has accepted the position of Riverton's high school teacher beginning in September," said Mr. Hodges. "She has experience, excellent qualifications, and the personal endorsement of Father Ogroski, senior priest of Saint Mary's Roman Catholic Church of

Chicago. I am very pleased to announce the acceptance of Miss Megan O'Brien to be Riverton's first high school teacher."

The congregation cheered; there was hugging, back slapping, and much talking. Buckley Hodges, Father O'Brien, and Reverend Wesley put their arms around each other's shoulders.

"We've got a teacher!" declared Reverend Wesley.

"Yes," smiled Father O'Brien. "Riverton has a high school teacher. And I will be reunited with my sister."

"Your sister!" exclaimed Reverend Wesley. The congregation was suddenly quiet again.

"Yes," said Father O'Brien, "my sister, Megan O'Brien."

"Is she a nun?" asked Reverend Wesley.

"No, she thought about the holy orders, but decided that was not the life for her."

Reverend Wesley gave a very short sermon, quickly finished the service, turned to Abby. "The closing hymn please."

After the closing hymn, the reverend said, "The Peace of the Lord be always with you," the people responded, "And also with you," and the service was over.

Brad, Audrey, Wilma Sue, and Buck met in front of the church. Detective Pulaski and Father O'Brien accepted Reverend Wesley's invitation to lunch at the Wesley's home.

"That was certainly a revelation!" said Buck. "I can't believe Father O'Brien's sister is going to be our high school teacher next year."

"Father O'Brien will probably want to have a house by the time his sister arrives," said Audrey.

"Another house-building," predicted Buck. "Just like the one we had for the Petrovs."

"Pa is waiting," said Wilma Sue. "I'll see you tomorrow."

Brad and Audrey watched as Wilma Sue got into the buggy. Buck got the nod from his father and said good-bye to Brad, Audrey, and Harry, as he climbed into his family's buckboard. Brad and Audrey walked slowly to the hitching rail, untethered their horses, and prepared to mount up.

"This has been a momentous Sunday morning," said Audrey. "First, the $3,000 reward for Jerry Chetham. Second, Miss Megan O'Brien will be our high school teacher next year. And third, we find out that she is Father O'Brien's sister!"

They mounted their horses and headed home at a walk. They were silent for several minutes, looking at the trees and listening to the chirping birds.

"We've already split the reward for the other gang members with Running Bear, his braves, and the other folks who helped us," said Brad. "That reward money will help pay for a house for Father O'Brien and his sister."

"Brad, this summer, I want to be able to sew and read this summer. I don't want to help you capture outlaws. So, if you see or hear something suspicious, get someone else to help you. Please."

Brad laughed. "I will do my best to meet your wishes."

Audrey leaned forward in her saddle. "Winner gets the biggest piece of pie?" asked Audrey.

"The biggest piece of pie," agreed Brad. "One, two, three!"

A NOTE ABOUT: "EASTER HYMN"

"Jesus Christ is Risen Today"

Reverend Charles Wesley (1707-1788) graduated from Oxford in 1729. He was ordained a priest in the Church of England, a.k.a. the Anglican Church or Episcopal Church, in 1735.

Charles Wesley produced about 6,500 hymns, including "Hark! The Herald Angels Sing," "Christ the Lord is Risen Today," and "Easter Hymn." "Easter Hymn" was first published as "The Resurrection" in *Lyra Davidica*, a 1708 hymnbook.

Wesley used the earliest known version of "The Resurrection" found in a 1478 German manuscript to write the version we sing today. He made it easier to sing by smoothing out the melody and text and by transposing it down from the key of D Major to the key of C Major, an easier range to sing.

Why is it easier to sing? Think of **F**, the top line of the treble clef, the highest note in the Bb version of the United States National Anthem, "The Star-Spangled Banner." This high note is a bit of a strain for most people to sing. Imagine having to go still higher, to an **F#,** to sing the highest note in the original D Major version of "Easter Hymn!" In **C** major, the highest note is an **E**.

Wesley re-titled "The Resurrection" as "Salisbury." It is also known by the titles "Easter Morn and "Worgan." Some hymnals vary the first line of the text to "Christ the Lord is Risen Today" rather than "Jesus Christ is Risen Today." Some hymnals use Wesley's text but set the music to a different melody. This cross matching of text and music was a common practice at the time and was not considered plagiarism. Examples include "Christ the Lord is Ris'n Today" with melody by Dresden and "Jesus Christ is Risen Today" with music by Robert Williams.

Wesley's "Easter Hymn" was published in his Foundery book, *A Collection of Tunes* in 1792, in Thomas Williams' *Psalmodia Evangelica: A Collection of Psalm and Hymn-Tunes* in 1789, and in *A Pocket Hymn Book* in 1793.

Although very close to his older brother, John Wesley, Charles remained a traditional Anglican throughout his life. John Wesley developed a less traditional **method** of preaching that included taking the Christian faith to the people via outdoor preaching and singing. His outdoor preaching **method**, which included singing Charles Wesley's hymns, was a forerunner of the revival meetings that swept the United States in the 1800s.

After John Wesley's death, Anglican priests and church members who liked John's method of preaching founded the Methodist Episcopal Church, now known as the United Methodist Church.

Charles Wesley's "Easter Hymn" continues to be sung in Christian churches around the world.

A NOTE ABOUT:
DWIGHT L. MOODY

Reverend Dwight L. Moody, the United States' leading 19th-century evangelist, was born in Northfield, Massachusetts on February 5, 1837. Four years later, his father died. The following month, his mother gave birth to twins, bringing the number of Moody children to nine: seven boys and two girls.

When Dwight was ten, he and his brothers were hired out to nearby farms to help with chores, earning money to help support their family. Seven years later, he decided he'd had enough of farm life and left for Boston.

After several penniless days wandering the streets of Boston, 17-year-old Moody began work as a sales clerk for his uncle, who required that he attend the Mount Vernon Congregational Church and Sunday school. A year later, in 1855, he was baptized in the church. Demonstrating a unique business sense, he quickly became his uncle's leading salesman.

The next year, Moody moved to Chicago, then a boom town burdened with vices of gambling, saloons, and prostitution. There his business skills earned him a weekly income of $30, six times higher than the average wage. As was common in Chicago at the time, he speculated in real estate and made short-term loans at high interest rates. He sent money to his family and made interest-free loans to his relatives.

His passion for Christianity led him to participate in several churches simultaneously: Plymouth Congregational Church, First Methodist Episcopal Church, and the First Baptist Church. Handing out tracts and Bibles, he met J. B. Stillson, a Presbyterian elder doing the same thing. They teamed up, and Stillson helped guide Moody in his evangelistic work.

In 1856 Moody started a mission for the orphaned children of 'Little Hell,' a slum just north of the Chicago River. To attract the children to his gospel meetings, his staff gave pennies or candy to those that came.

His hardy constitution required only five to six hours' sleep a night, allowing him time to conduct evening gospel meetings for children. By this time in his business career, Moody was earning $5,000 a year, ten times the average wage.

By the fall of 1860, attendance at Moody's gospel meetings for impoverished children reached 1,500 a week. President-elect Lincoln visited one of Moody's meetings in Little Hell and encouraged them to listen and learn. A few months later, when President Lincoln called for 75,000 three-month Army volunteers at the outbreak of the Civil War, 75 students and teachers at Moody's mission were the first to enlist.

On March 4, 1861, Lincoln was inaugurated as President of the United States. By then, seven southern states had seceded and formed the Confederate States of America. On the 12th of April, Fort Sumpter was attacked by South Carolina troops. Three days later on 15 April, the United States declared war on the Confederate States of America.

By the end of April, in response to President Lincoln's request, the 72nd Illinois Volunteer Regiment had been formed and was stationed at Camp Douglas, a few miles south of Chicago. Its men asked Moody to become their chaplain. Moody visited the regiment, as well as other regiments at the camp. He saw liquor, gambling, and other vices stealing the soldiers' time, health, and money.

He responded by printing and distributing hymnals to each regiment. The Christian Association erected tents for Moody, who held eight to ten gospel meetings a day in response to the regiments' requests. He recruited clergy and lay people to staff the tents as additional units arrived. In 1862, 9,000 Confederate prisoners were held at Camp Douglas; Moody and his team took the gospel to the prisoners.

Influential men who worked with Moody included many successful and well-known men.

- *Cyrus McCormick (farm equipment manufacturer)
- John Wanamaker (founder of the Wanamaker drug store chain)
- Lord Kinnaird (steamships)
- Frances Willard (Women's Christian Temperance Union)
- Phillips Brooks (the Episcopal priest who wrote "O Little Town of Bethlehem" and preached once for Moody when Moody couldn't make a meeting)
- George Stuart (banker)
- Ira Sankey (vocalist, hymnist, and music publisher)

- Franklin Fairbanks (scales)
- Booker T. Washington (educator, founder of Tuskegee Institute)
- Philip Armour (meat packing)
- Gustavus F. Swift (Swift & Company, meat packing)
- Flemming H. Revell (publisher)

Moody's simple half-hour sermons differed from the hour-and-a-half sermons of other ministers and priests. He preached God's love, rather than God's judgment. He led the people to the Lord; he didn't frighten them to the Lord. He persuaded his listeners to look at themselves, consider their position with God, and to accept Jesus.

A committee of Christian businessmen used the royalties and profits from the sale of books, tracts, and donations to fund Moody's church and other Christian organizations.

Moody was extremely perceptive. Something about an usher at an 1876 revival meeting in Chicago disturbed him. He expressed his concern to the revival's chairman and was later informed that the usher's name was Charles J. Guiteau. Five years later, on 2 July 1881, Guiteau, a mentally ill man who was frustrated that he did not receive a job from the president, assassinated the President of the United States, James Garfield.

Moody pushed successfully for students of all races and denominations to attend his seminaries. Moody's Northfield and Mount Hermon seminaries promoted tolerance and acceptance of non-Protestant Christianity and Judaism at a time when discrimination against Catholics and Jews was common. Students came from conservative and liberal backgrounds, from Catholic, Baptist, Methodist, Episcopal, Independent, and the Church of Christ denominations.

Prominent among the many reasons for Moody's success as an evangelist was his presentation of Christianity and the Bible, in simple terms, for the common man.

BRAD AND THE PINKERTONS
RESCUE AUDREY!

FOR AN EXCERPT, TURN THE PAGE.

CHAPTER 1

Tuesday, 7 June 1881: "I hope you can get us a good room in Denver, Ma," said Audrey, turning away from the stagecoach. "Brad and I will take care of the bags."

"I'll take good care of Brad and Audrey, Mrs. Benton," promised Deputy Sheriff Dan Black. Abigail Benton, Abby to most everyone, left the stage office and headed toward the hotel.

"I'll stack our bags by the wall," said Brad, but he stopped, a bag in hand, looking intently at the door of the bank next door to the stage office.

Two men ran out of the bank, guns drawn, and mounted their horses, which were standing close to the stagecoach. Two more men with drawn guns followed them out of the bank.

"Get down, Audrey! They're robbing the bank," warned Brad, pulling his sister down onto the boardwalk with him.

"It's a lawman! Get him," shouted one of the robbers through his mask, as he pointed his pistol at Dan Black.

"I'll get him!" yelled another robber, taking a couple of shots at the deputy sheriff.

Dan Black started shooting at the robbers from the boardwalk. A third robber was the first to get hit, as he mounted his horse. The man dropped his pistol, clutched at his saddle horn, and fell to the street.

As the deputy was taking aim at another one of the robbers, a bullet from one of the robber's pistol struck him. The deputy fell to his knees, but he held on to his pistol. Taking careful aim, the wounded deputy shot back.

"I'm hit," yelped another of the robbers, clutching his side. "But I'll make it. Let's go."

The three men spurred their horses to a gallop down the street, taking the fallen robber's riderless horse with them.

Brad watched them gallop away and rushed to Deputy Black, who was now flat on his back on the boardwalk. Pulling off his kerchief, Brad pressed it to the wound, stopping the bleeding.

"I'll help this one!" Audrey shouted to her brother, removing the wounded robber's kerchief and then pressing it against his wound. "What's your name?"

"Virgil."

"Virgil," said Audrey, "I have to remove your gunbelt. It's obstructing the wound." Audrey unbuckled the gunbelt and pulled it free. Picking up the pistol, she pushed it into its holster and placed it by her side, away from Virgil's reach. "Don't move; we'll get you to a doctor as soon as we can."

"Careful, lady! My partners are coming," he groaned as he reached for her. "I don't want you to get hurt."

Seven other men, guns drawn, rushed out of the bank and mounted their horses. Another robber looked through his mask at the two men lying in the street as Brad and Audrey bent over them.

"She's got Virgil's gun," shouted a robber, pointing his pistol toward Audrey. "I'll get her."

Audrey heard the shot and felt a bullet whiz past her. "Don't shoot!" she shouted. "I'm helping your partner. He's hurt pretty bad." Virgil didn't wait for another shot; he limply raised his arm, waved to his partners, and pulled Audrey down beside him.

"I'll get the hero helping the deputy," said one of them trying to aim his pistol and control his frightened mount at the same time.

Brad heard the first bullet whiz past, so he quickly fell to the ground. As he fell, a second slug ripped through his shirt, gouged his side, and buried itself in the street.

A ripple of gunfire erupted from the bank as one the bank's customers, rancher Brett Grimes, began shooting at the escaping robbers.

A robber teetered back on his skittering mount, dropping his pistol as he fell to the dusty street. Another of the rancher's bullets found its mark, and one more robber clutched his side. The wounded man gripped his horse's reins as he held his side, staring at Audrey. Another robber, his trousers wet with blood from a bullet in the thigh, grabbed the reins of his partner's riderless horse.

The gang's leader, heard the rancher's gunfire, drew his six-shooter, and fired back. During the exchange of gunfire, one of the rancher's bullets hit the kerchief masking the leader's face, knocking it down. His six-shooter empty, the rancher wisely ducked back into the bank for cover.

Audrey raised her head as the gunfire closed and

her eyes met the gang leader's. His cold, emotionless eyes stared at Audrey as he pulled his kerchief back up. She shivered as their eyes briefly met.

"Come on, let's get out of here!" shouted a robber, spurring his horse down the street. "Virgil and Jesse are gone." The remaining robbers galloped after him, leaving Brad and Audrey bent over two wounded men. The third man lay sprawled in the street, bleeding.

♘

"I'd like three beds," said Abby. "That can be one room or two rooms; I have my son and daughter with me."

"I'm short of rooms," replied the clerk, "but I can give you one large room, with two beds. It's a corner room, in the shape of an L. That's the best I can do."

"I understand, said Abby, "that will do. I'm here for ten days; I'm studying with Percival Vaughan-Williams, the organist at the Episcopal Church."

"Yes, a superb musician. You may be playing at his recital on the 16th of June. My name is George Girard, I sing in his choir."

"Why, that sounds like gun shots!" exclaimed Abby, turning her head toward the door.

There were a couple of thuds, and a piece of woodwork splintered above the clerk's head. "On the floor!" he shouted. "Everyone get on the floor!"

"They're robbing the bank!" yelled a man running through the door. He looked around the lobby, and then quickly hid behind a large chair.

"Who's robbing the bank, Nyle? which bank?" shouted George Girard from behind the counter.

"The bank by the stage office," yelled Nyle. "And

there's a young blond lady and a dark-haired young man treating the wounded."

"My children!" screamed Abby, getting to her feet as another bullet thudded into the hotel door. "Those are my children treating the wounded!"

A large man quickly stood up, grabbed Abby, and pulled her back down to the floor, covering her with his body. Several more bullets thudded into the hotel lobby, as gunfire and screams of horses broke the afternoon's tranquility.

"You can't help your children if you get yourself shot, Ma'am. Wait until the shooting is over. I'm sure your children are doing everything you and your husband taught them to do in a dangerous situation."

"I'm sure they are, Mr. ...?" said Abby, waiting for the man to tell her his name.

"William, William Crawford," he replied. "And your name, Ma'am?"

"Abigail Benton. And my children do know what to do in a dangerous situation, but they've never been in the middle of a gun battle, although their father has."

"Civil War, I presume, Mrs. Benton."

"You presume correctly."

"And you?"

"Civil War, Union Army," he replied.

They heard more gunfire, then the clatter of approaching horses as the robbers galloped down the street. When the sound faded away the hotel guests slowly got to their feet.

"Thank you, Mr. Crawford," said Abby, standing up, "but now I must check on my children."

Abby picked up the hem of her dress, rushed out

the door and ran down the boardwalk to the stage depot. She saw men coming out of the bank, the stage depot, and surrounding businesses. In the middle of the street she saw Audrey, her blond hair glistening in the sunlight, bent over a man sprawled in the street. Not far away, she saw Brad, his hand pressed against the side of a man lying on the boardwalk. But worse, she saw blood on the side of her son's shirt.

OTHER TITLES BY THIS AUTHOR

THE BIGFOOT GANG

CAPTIVE

FIERY BLIZZARD

HEALER GANG

DENVER MUSIC

ABOUT THE AUTHOR

Born and raised in the West, Smith grew up where many farmers still used horses to plow their fields. Steam engines were the norm for railroads, and a diesel locomotive was quite an event. He's now caught up with modern civilization.

After serving in the U. S. Air Force, he later worked as a teacher, professional musician, and federal employee. He has now settled down and lives in Virginia. You can find out more about him at www.edgsmith.com.

CONNECT WITH THE AUTHOR

Website:
www.edgsmith.com

Social Media:
www.facebook.com/edgsmith

ACKNOWLEDGEMENTS:

Many thanks to Lora Cooper for her editing, suggestions and helping to bring The Healer Gang to completion. Lora is a museum educator who lives and works in Charlottesville, Virginia. She holds a B.A. in History from Christopher Newport University and a Master of Education from the University of Virginia. Lora has sung with school and church choirs for many years and occasionally records acapella pieces with friends. And to paraphrase a quote attributed to Winston Churchill, Lora identified some grammarizing up with which she would not put. And thanks to Kathryn Boudreau, and her dog Daisy, for taking photos and providing encouragement